SUPERB WRITING
TO FIRE THE IMAGINATION

Louise Cooper writes:

Years ago, on a visit to East Anglia, I saw two old churches. They stood side by side and they were identical – except for the fact that one was whole and clearly used, while the other was a crumbling ruin. I can't recall exactly where they were, and I glimpsed them only briefly, through a car window. But the memory stayed in my mind, and with it a haunting question. Why *two* churches? What made the people of the time abandon one, and build another close by? The explanation is probably simple and straightforward – but writers are never satisfied with that. My imagination was fired; I invented strange and spine-chilling possibilities . . . and now, long afterwards, one of those ideas has inspired the story of *Hunter's Moon*. I'm sure that my tale is nothing like the truth, and that's just as well. But the eerie, elusive memory of those two ancient buildings still sends a ghost of a shive down my spine . . .

Other titles available from Louise Cooper:

Daughter of Storms
The Dark Caller
Keepers of Light

Mirror Mirror 1: Breaking Through
Mirror Mirror 2: Running Free
Mirror Mirror 3: Testing Limits

Demon Crossing

HUNTER'S MOON

LOUISE COOPER

**Hodder
Children's
Books**

A division of Hodder Headline Limited

This edition published in 2003
by Hodder Children's Books Limited

10 9 8 7 6 5 4 3 2 1

A Catalogue record for this book is available from
the British Library

ISBN 0 340 85400 6

Typeset in Bembo by Avon DataSet Ltd,
Bidford-on-Avon, Warwickshire

Printed and bound in Great Britain by
Bookmarque Ltd, Croydon, Surrey

Hodder Children's Books
A Division of Hodder Headline Limited
338 Euston Road
London NW1 3BH

1

'I don't want to go home,' Bridget Chandler declared sourly. She had twisted herself into an impossible angle on the car seat and was peering backwards with her face pressed against the window, trying to get a last glimpse of the sea. 'Why can't we just stay at Nan's for ever and ever?'

Her sister, Gil, who was five years older, nudged her hard in the ribs. 'Biddy, stop kicking me! Course we can't stay at Nan's for ever. I don't know what you're moaning about, anyway – we've still got another week to go before school starts again.'

'Two *whole weeks*!' Biddy mocked. 'Big deal! If we lived at Nan's—'

Their father whipped round from the front passenger seat. 'Well we don't, and any more than two weeks of you would probably finish Nan off! Now shut up, the pair of you, and let Mum concentrate.'

He turned round again and Biddy pulled a grotesque face at his back view. Gil said, 'Dad's got the rats. He doesn't want to go home, either.'

'It's not that, it's 'cause Mum's driving.' Biddy bounced on the seat. 'Dad always gets the rats when Mum drives. He thinks she's going to crash the car and kill us all!'

'I most certainly do not!' Mr Chandler snapped. 'Your mother's a very good driver.'

Mrs Chandler muttered something about Dad being a hypocrite, and changed gear for a bend. Gil, knowing that their father was starting to get very irritable, nudged Biddy hard and hissed at her to be quiet. Biddy sighed in a martyred way and screwed round to look out of the window again. Now that they were on the country lanes there wasn't much to see; only high hedgerows skimming by, with the huge blue bowl of the Norfolk sky beyond. Sheringham was a long way behind them, and if they *were* still anywhere near the coast then the sea was invisible. She sighed again, slumped back in the seat and started to unwrap a bar of chocolate. Gil, watching, was just about to say, 'You get that on my jeans and you're dead,' when Mr Chandler spoke.

'Jean, are you *sure* we should have gone left and not right at the diversion?'

Mrs Chandler's eyes in the driving mirror were suddenly hard. 'Of course I'm sure!'

'OK, if you say so.' A pause. 'But I could have sworn that last signpost we passed said Neapham.'

'Neapham?' Mrs Chandler's voice went up the scale and the car wobbled alarmingly. She got it back under control and added, 'You can't have read it properly. We're nowhere near Neapham; it's miles out of our way, right back on the coast.'

'All right,' Mr Chandler responded with an edge in

his voice. 'But you know what the map said—'

'I know what *you* said. But then you've never been the world's best map-reader, have you?'

Gil and Biddy exchanged a glance and both raised their eyebrows. It was always the same; when their father drove and their mother read the map everything was fine, but when it was the other way round the sparks soon started flying.

'Look,' Mrs Chandler said sharply, 'there's another turning up ahead. I'll pull in to the verge and you can have a good look and see who's right. Will that make you happy?'

Her husband didn't answer. The car slowed as they neared the turning, and he wound down the window to read the faded old signpost planted in the long verge-side grass. Gil and Biddy peered forward, too, and after a few seconds three pairs of accusing eyes focused on Mrs Chandler.

'Oh, b—' Then she stopped herself before she could say something extremely rude. 'That's *ridiculous*. I *know* I took the right road!'

'And I know I read the map accurately.' There was a definite hint of I-told-you-so in their dad's voice. 'But oh no, you wouldn't have it.' He looked at his watch. 'If we hadn't gone wrong we'd have been on the A47 by now.'

'Well we did and we aren't. It's all the fault of those blasted road-works, sending traffic round by the long

3

way.' Savagely Mrs Chandler yanked the car into gear again and something made a dreadful grinding noise. Mr Chandler winced. 'Well, we'll take the next right turning we can find, and if we get home an hour or two late that's just too bad.'

'An hour or two?' Biddy sat bolt upright. 'Oh, Mum! I'm starving to death already! *And* I want to go to the loo,' she added as an afterthought.

'You can't possibly,' her mother told her. 'You went just before we left Nan's.'

'Well, I want to go again.'

Gil glowered at her sister. She was starting to get tired of this. First Mum and Dad bickering and now Biddy sticking her oar in. Gil hadn't wanted the holiday to end, either, but she was sensible enough to know that they couldn't stay in Sheringham for ever, and anyway she'd begun to miss being surrounded by her own things and her own friends. All she really wanted now was to get home as quickly as possible, but before she could say so, her father cut in.

'Jean, isn't Neapham the place where you used to go when you were little?'

She frowned at him. 'Yes, it is. But I haven't been back there for more than twenty years, and I can't say I ever want to. There's nothing there except the village and the beach. Why?'

'Well . . . It's only a couple of miles, according to the signpost. And if Biddy really is going to be a pest we'll

4

have to find somewhere to stop.' Mr Chandler looked over his shoulder and winked at the girls. 'What do you think? Shall we have a last look at the sea, and check out the place where Mum spent her wild and reckless youth?'

Biddy crowed delightedly, and Gil said, 'Oh, yes! Come on, Mum, please – it needn't take long.'

'We might be able to get some food,' Mr Chandler added.

'I doubt it. The place'll be like a graveyard.'

'Oh, come on. There must be a pub where we can get something to eat, and it'll be better than fish and chips or pizzas to take home.' He reached across and tugged at a lock of her hair. 'Or have you got some guilty secret waiting for you that you don't want me to find out about?'

She batted his hand away but her mouth was twitching with amusement. 'Oh, all right, then. I suppose it'll be interesting to see how much the old place has changed. But don't blame me if you're all disappointed.'

The girls yelped in excitement and approval as she let off the brake and turned the car left on to the Neapham road. It was more of a lane really, with blind corners and hardly any passing places; Mrs Chandler drove slowly, peering ahead and hooting before the bends, and Biddy started to chant, 'We're going to see the sea again, the sea, the sea, the sea!' until Mr Chandler told her to shut up.

'Didn't you used to stay with a relative round here?' he asked Mum when they reached a straight stretch and she could relax. 'An uncle or something?'

'Alan Granger, you mean?' She changed gear. 'Yes. He's my mum's older brother. We lost touch years ago, though.'

'Wonder if he's still there?'

Her mouth set in an odd, hard line. 'He wouldn't have moved. He was the local doctor; they treated him like Lord High Everything Else in the village, and he wouldn't give that up. But before you say another word, we are *not* going to drop in on him. For a start I don't suppose he even remembers me, and for another thing his house gave me the creeps. Horrible place; dark and gloomy. I always had nightmares when I stayed there. No wonder his daughter – my cousin Rose – turned out weird.'

'Is that our Auntie Rose?' Biddy piped up.

'Sort of.'

'Why haven't we ever met her?' Biddy was very partial to uncles and aunts; they could always be relied on to give you money when you visited them.

'Because I haven't seen her for years and years, since long before Dad and I even met,' her mother said. 'She got married and moved to Yorkshire. Anyway, you wouldn't like her any more than you'd like your Great-Uncle Alan.'

And that, it seemed, was as much as Mrs Chandler wanted to say about her mysterious relations. They drove on, until suddenly Biddy let out an ear-piercing shriek.

'*There's the sea!*'

There indeed it was, a great, shining ribbon of blue brilliance, stretching across the horizon ahead as the hedgerows opened out and they entered the village of Neapham. The village itself sprawled along the edge of an expanse of sand dunes, that led in turn to a huge swathe of golden, sandy beach, reaching away in both directions as far as the eye could see. Biddy howled with delight and kicked her feet in the air, and even Gil whooped at the sight of such gloriously empty perfection.

'You are a pair of idiots!' Mrs Chandler said, but she was laughing as she slowed the car down and finally stopped at the T-junction where the village road crossed the lane. 'Though I've got to admit, I'd forgotten how beautiful this beach is.'

Mr Chandler grinned at her. 'Pleased we came?'

'Yes. Yes, I am.' Then she looked over her shoulder. 'Right, you two. What do you want to do?'

'Go on the beach, oh, let's go on the beach!' Biddy pleaded. 'I want to run and run and *run*!'

'OK. Then we'll drive down to the Anchor – if it's still there.' Mrs Chandler looked surprised and pleased with herself at remembering the name of the village's pub. 'It's right on the dunes and there's a car park.' She eyed Biddy sternly. 'And a loo.'

She turned left and drove along the village street, which seemed to consist of nothing but terraces of little flint houses and one shop, closed and shuttered. The pub was just beyond the last house, standing on its own patch of hard-packed sand on the opposite side of the road. To Mrs Chandler's dismay it wasn't called the Anchor any more but the Shoals of Herring Bar, and there were lights strung round it and a sign proclaiming 'Burgers – Pizzas – Scampi'.

'Never mind,' Mr Chandler said as they pulled in to the car park. 'At least they've got tables outside. We can sit there and enjoy the view.'

She nodded and switched off the engine. The change was eerie; a thump of music came faintly from the pub but it was almost eclipsed by the whistle and whisper of wind in the sand dunes, and beyond that there was a sense of enormous silence. For a brief moment Gil felt a strange, cold prickling, like kittens' claws up the length of her spine. Then the peculiar feeling vanished as Biddy pushed open the car door on the other side.

'Come on, Gil! Let's go and look at the beach!'

Gil scrambled after her. Mrs Chandler called out, 'Stay where we can see you, Biddy!' and Mr Chandler added, 'Twenty minutes, no more!' Then the dunes were in front of them and they were ploughing into the soft, silver-tinted sand, running between tussocks of coarse grass and on to the gentle slope down to the beach.

'Ohh!' Biddy slithered to a halt where the dunes gave way to the hard-packed sand of the high tideline. 'It's *brill*!'

8

Gil drew in a deep breath, sucking the wonderful air into her lungs. Salt and brine and seaweed; the tide was low and the waves hissed as they rolled in, their tops glittering in the westering sun. To right and left the empty beach stretched away into a bright haze, and the sand shone like silver, broken only by the occasional dark wedges of wooden groynes sloping down from the dunes towards the water.

'There's just no one here.' Biddy's voice was awed. 'No one at *all*, not for miles and miles. It's as if we were the only people in the whole world!' She danced on the spot, kicking up sand. 'Gil, just think if we lived here! We could have horses! We could ride them along the beach every day, galloping like the wind!'

Biddy had never been on a horse in her life, but at the moment they were her great obsession. 'Come on, Gil, let's pretend!' She was like a wild horse herself, and nothing could hold her back. 'Let's pretend we're riding the fastest horses in the world, and gallop away!'

She was off before Gil could say another word, racing along the sand, jumping and leaping, hands flapping and smacking against her sides like a jockey, spurring her mount on to a famous victory. Gil stared after her for a few moments. She was much too old to charge around like a crazy kid, but part of her wanted to whoop and yell and run and join in too. Pushing away the feeling and telling herself she was a complete idiot, she turned and looked out over the ocean, to where the vastness of the North Sea met the vastness of the sky and everything merged into a blue-grey haze.

'*Gil!*' Biddy's voice floated back on the wind like the distant, shrill cry of a seagull. Forgetting their mother's injunction to stay within sight she was already a hundred metres away, jumping the first groyne, turning to wave her arms eagerly. 'Gil, come and gallop!'

Gil glanced back at the pub. Their parents had disappeared inside and no one was watching her.

'I'm coming!' she yelled, and started to sprint along the sand in her sister's wake.

Biddy knew it wouldn't be long before Gil caught up with her. That was the worst thing about having an older sister; Gil had longer legs and could run much faster, so whenever they raced – and that wasn't often, because Gil hardly ever would – Biddy always lost. This time, though, she was determined to outwit her sister, and when she saw Gil jump the second of the groynes and come pounding after her she veered inland towards the sand dunes. The dunes were great; Biddy could lay a false trail of footprints in the soft sand then hide behind a tussock of grass, and when Gil started looking for her she'd jump out and give her the fright of her life.

In her imagination Biddy was still riding a horse. She snorted and whinnied – quite convincingly, she thought – as she made her way among the dunes, looking for a good place to hide. The wind had dropped and it was very quiet, and when she looked up she realised that she must have run a long way along the beach. She looked around. There was a belt of stunted and scrubby pine trees behind the dunes, then the road, then more trees, and . . . something else.

Curious, Biddy peered harder, and saw that beyond the second line of trees was an old church with a wall around it. Something about it seemed wrong somehow, and that puzzled her until, after a few moments, she realised what it was. The church was a ruin. The roof had fallen in, the squat, square tower gaped open to the blue sky, and what had once been a neatly-tended churchyard was now a thicket of brambles and couch-grass. A few old, mossy gravestones poked up from the tangle here and there, but the place had an air of desolation that drove all notions of horses and hiding from Biddy's mind.

She walked towards the road. She wouldn't cross over – she wasn't allowed to cross roads on her own and it was one of the few orders she didn't argue with – but if she went a bit further along on this side she'd get a much better view of the ruin. Then, as the scrubby trees thinned out, she saw the second church.

It stood beyond the ruin, separated from it by a stone wall, and Biddy's eyes widened in astonishment as she looked harder. The two churches were absolutely identical. The only difference between them was that the second church still had its roof and tower intact, and the churchyard wasn't a tangled wilderness but neat and tended and tidy. *Weird*, Biddy thought. Where had Gil got to? She'd love this.

She turned to call out to her sister and urge her to hurry up and see the strange thing for herself. And came face to face with a boy.

Biddy yelped in shock and almost fell over as she jumped back a pace. 'Where did *you* come from?'

The boy was a year or two older than her, and the most striking thing about him was the colour of his hair. It was red – fiery red – and it was the first time Biddy had ever encountered anyone with hair so like her own and Gil's. The sisters suffered, as they saw it, from the same problem. At school they were both saddled with the nickname of 'Carrots'. Biddy shrugged it off, but Gil hated it. That was why she had begged Mum to let her have it cut so short. When she got to be Gil's age, Biddy thought, she'd probably feel the same; and as no one else in the family had hair like theirs it really didn't seem fair. But now she was confronted by a complete stranger who was another Carrots, and despite the start he'd given her, she felt a wave of fellow-feeling.

She added, 'Sorry; I didn't mean to yell. You made me jump, that's all.'

The boy didn't answer but only stood staring at her. He was very thin, she noticed, and very pale, too. No freckles like she and Gil had, and his skin looked as if he spent most of his time shut away from the light.

Trying again, Biddy asked, 'Are you from the village? Naffam, or whatever it's called?'

'What if we are?' The boy's voice snapped out so suddenly that it startled her. 'That's our business, not yours.' He had a thick accent that was hard to understand, but the fierce contempt in his tone was clear enough, and Biddy bristled.

'I only asked!' She glowered at him. 'Anyway, what do you mean, *our* business? I can only see one of you!'

The boy glanced over his shoulder towards the dunes, and to Biddy's surprise a girl emerged from behind a tall tussock of grass. She was younger than the boy; she had red hair, too, and she was wearing a shapeless top and a baggy skirt that was much too long for her. Her feet were bare and sandy, and Biddy couldn't help noticing that her toenails needed cutting. The girl stood beside the boy and took hold of his hand, staring uneasily at Biddy. Her eyes were very bright blue but somehow very sad, and instinctively Biddy felt sorry for her.

She said, 'Hi,' hoping the girl would be more friendly than the boy. 'This beach is great, isn't it? I was being a horse. What are you two doing here?'

The girl didn't return her smile. 'We're waiting,' she said in a soft, accented voice. 'We always come here, me and my brother. We always come. To wait.'

Biddy frowned. 'Who for?'

'Our father. He'll be coming home by sea, so we wait here every evening and look for his ship.'

'Where's he coming home from?' Biddy asked.

The girl didn't answer, but her blue eyes suddenly lit up in a strange, almost manic way. 'He must come soon,' she said passionately. 'He *must*.'

Biddy began to feel uneasy. The girl's tone was weird, and that look in her eyes . . . She took a step back towards the beach. 'Look, I'd better go. My sister'll be wondering where I am . . .'

The boy laughed. It was an extraordinary laugh, sharp and cruel, and as Biddy's eyes widened he said coldly, 'Yes, go. Go on, go away. It's too late for us. Go away, before it's too late for you as well.'

His tone and his words really frightened Biddy, and she stumbled back three more paces. 'OK, OK, I'm going! There's no need to be—' And she stopped as she saw that his expression had abruptly changed and he was looking past her to a spot behind her left shoulder.

Biddy spun round. The sun was beginning to set, and the last rays slanted across the tangle of shrubbery around the old church, casting long shadows. Just for a moment one of those shadows seemed to move.

The boy hissed at her, softly but savagely, '*Before it's too late!*' Biddy's heart jumped under her ribs and she turned back again—

The boy and girl had vanished.

Behind her, on the other side of the narrow lane, something rustled in the brambles . . .

★ ★ ★

14

'Biddy?' Gil ploughed through the soft sand, breathless and cross. Where *was* she? 'Biddy! Stop messing around – come out!'

Still Biddy didn't answer. Gil said something under her breath, then headed for one of the higher dunes, which would give her a better vantage point. The dry, soft sand was hard to climb and kept slithering back in small avalanches, so it took her some while to scramble to the top. Hot, panting and furious, she stared around. No Biddy. There was a belt of trees behind the dunes, between the beach and the lane. Could she have gone over there? The silly fool knew she wasn't allowed to cross roads on her own . . . Gil peered, but the sunset light dazzled her and she saw nothing.

She shouted again. 'Bid-*DY*! I've had enough of this! If you don't come out by the time I count to three, I'll—'

The threat cut off as, turning, she saw an out-of-place splash of bright blue beside a neighbouring dune. Biddy's sandals were blue . . .

Gil slithered down the slope and broke into a run. Skidding round the curve of the dune, she saw her sister.

Biddy lay on her back in the sand. Her eyes were closed and there was a funny little smile on her face. For one moment Gil almost believed she was shamming. But then she saw the terrible, feverish flush on Biddy's cheeks.

'Biddy!' Gil dropped to her knees and shook the little girl, gently at first then more violently. But it was useless.

Biddy was unconscious. God, was she even *breathing*? Yes – her chest was rising and falling, but the movement was so slight that it was barely visible. And Gil was terrified that any moment it might stop.

She jumped to her feet and looked wildly around. There was no one in sight, no one who might help, and only her own and Biddy's footprints led back to the beach. Fighting the panic that welled up in her stomach and made her want to be sick, Gil stumbled back the way she'd come, and as she started to run along the beach she waved her arms towards the distant pub and yelled at the top of her voice,

'*Mum! Dad! Oh, Mum, help! HELP!*'

2

'What do you mean, you don't know?' Mrs Chandler's face was dead white and her voice started to rise hysterically as she confronted the doctor. 'You *must* know! Children don't just collapse like that without some good reason! For God's sake, *what's wrong with my daughter?*'

The doctor did her best to be calm and reassuring. 'Mrs Chandler, please – we're running some tests now, and I'm sure we'll know all we need to in a few hours.'

'A few *hours?*' she echoed, shrill and incredulous. Mr Chandler laid a hand on her arm. 'Jean—'

She threw him off furiously. 'Don't "Jean" me! Don't *speak* to me! That's my child she's talking about, my *Biddy*!' She burst into tears.

Gil was guiltily thankful when someone came and shepherded her away from the office, to a small, quiet room with old but comfortable chairs in it. The nurse who had accompanied her offered a cup of tea.

'No, really – thanks, but I don't want anything.' Gil looked briefly at the nurse's sympathetic face then turned quickly away. 'I'm OK.'

'Well, at least sit down.' The nurse paused. 'It's your little sister, is it, who's been brought in?'

Gil nodded miserably. 'I was the one who found her.'

17

'That must have been awful. What happened? Did she fall and hit her head?'

'I don't know.' Gil glanced at the door, back towards the office from where, faintly, she could still hear her mother's upraised voice. 'She isn't cut anywhere, or anything. She's just unconscious. The doctor says they don't know what's wrong with her yet. That's why Mum . . . well, you know.' She waved a hand helplessly.

'Of course, I understand. Don't worry; we'll look after Biddy and do everything we can for her. And I expect the doctor'll give your mum a sedative. She'll be all right once she gets over the first shock.' Another pause. 'Do you live near here?'

'No,' Gil told her. 'We're from Hertfordshire. We've been staying with my nan in Sheringham; we were on our way home and we stopped to see the place where Mum used to spend her holidays when she was little.' Her mouth twisted suddenly. 'It was supposed to bring back happy memories.'

'Oh. I see.' The nurse looked thoughtful. 'Well, Sheringham's a bit of a way from here . . . Look, pet, would you wait here for me a moment?'

She went briskly out, and Gil sat staring dismally at her own feet and trying hard not to think about anything, least of all Biddy. It seemed an age but in fact was only a couple of minutes before the nurse came back, and when she did, Mr Chandler was with her.

'Gil?' He came over to her chair and planted a kiss on

the top of her head. 'Mum's having a lie-down; the doctor's given her something.'

Gil turned a pale, desperate face up to him. 'What about Biddy?'

'Well, as the doctor said, they're going to run some tests, but they won't know much more than they do now until tomorrow. So that leaves us in a bit of a jam. We can't stay here – the hospital hasn't got facilities for relatives – so we're going to have to work out what to do.'

'Couldn't we go back to Nan's?'

Dad shook his head. 'It's too far. We need to be nearby, in case . . .' His voice tailed off and he ran his hands distractedly through his hair. 'So I thought about Mum's Uncle Alan. He doesn't live very far from here. Maybe he could put us up for a bit.' He suddenly looked very tired and old. 'I mean, we can't go home. Not now.'

How they found the number Gil didn't know; maybe her mother knew it or maybe there weren't many Grangers in the local phone book, but within half an hour everything was settled. Someone had spoken to her great-uncle, and he immediately insisted that they must all come straight to his house, which was only a few miles away, and stay for as long as they wanted to. For Gil, the sudden arrival of a new player on the stage was unexpected and upsetting. Great-Uncle Alan was a complete stranger, and the thought of going to an unfamiliar house, meeting unfamiliar people and having to sleep under their roof, made her feel very insecure.

The three of them left the hospital. Mrs Chandler was glassy-eyed and seemed unable to walk properly, Dad had his arm around her shoulders, and Gil trailed along behind them. She was thankful to be shut into the car's familiar surroundings, away from the cream-painted corridors and hospital smell. But Biddy wasn't there. Biddy, who had grumbled and kicked and bounced around on the seat all the way from Sheringham, was lying back there in a lonely bed, still and silent . . .

Gil clenched a fist and bit her knuckles until the pain broke into her misery and made it recede. Mr Chandler was driving, white-faced, and Mrs Chandler was staring out of the window but seeing nothing. Neither of them seemed to be aware of Gil, and they didn't notice when her face crumpled and tears started to roll down her cheeks, so hot and salty and fast and uncontrollable that she thought they would never, ever stop.

April House was only two miles from Neapham, but in the pitch dark of a Norfolk night it might as well have been on another planet. Mr Chandler negotiated the lanes cautiously, following the directions he'd been given at the hospital, but they met no other cars and passed only an occasional isolated and unlit house set back from the road. It seemed to Gil that the only illumination anywhere in the world was the headlights, stabbing into the blackness ahead. She had stopped crying, but she almost wished that the tears were still there to blur the sight of the roadside hedge branches, looming and lurching like hideous, gnarled hands reaching for the car. Darkness didn't normally scare Gil, but tonight, cocooned with only a small metal box between herself and the hugeness of the night, she felt vulnerable and afraid, and desperately wanted the journey to end.

It did end at last. Gil felt the car slow down, and peered through the window just in time to glimpse a hand-painted sign that read *April House Only* before they swung off the road and were bumping down a lane that was hardly more than a narrow track lined by encroaching trees. Jolting and lurching in the ruts, the car rocked along for a hundred metres or so; then very softly Mrs Chandler said, 'Oh, my God . . .'

The trees had ended and April House stood silhouetted against a sky suddenly open and silvered with moonlight. It looked like a solid block of darkness, chimneys and gables jutting upwards at cruel angles; a huge, black, alien animal waiting to pounce. Lights shone in some of the windows but they only made the effect worse, for they were like mindless eyes glaring down. A sense of panic clutched at Gil's stomach and began to work its way up towards her throat. She thought: *We can't stay here, not this place, not here.*

'It hasn't changed a bit.' Mrs Chandler's voice cut in, and her tone was so bitter that Gil was jerked back to earth with a shock that set her heart racing. 'It's a Gothic monstrosity! And Alan hasn't done a single thing to make it any less repulsive. That's typical of him. He always was selfish!'

Her husband sighed, sounding more tired than Gil had ever heard him before. 'Well, we're here now; it's too late to change our minds.' He sucked in a breath. 'Haven't we got enough to worry about already, for God's sake, without you picking holes in something as trivial as what the house looks like?'

She didn't answer. They came to a halt in front of the house; the car engine died, and suddenly they were wrapped in grim silence. For a few moments nothing stirred. Mrs Chandler went on staring at the house, her lips set in a tight, painful line. Mr Chandler looked blindly at the steering wheel, and Gil fidgeted uneasily, wanting to break the ugly atmosphere between her parents but not knowing where to begin.

Then a new and much brighter light came on in the house's ornate porch. The front door opened, and a shadow loomed out across the pool of brightness.

'Jean? Is that you?'

Mrs Chandler hissed, 'Who the hell does he *think* it is?' which for some inexplicable reason – hysteria, perhaps – made Gil want to start laughing. Mr Chandler sighed and opened the door.

'Yes. Yes, it's us.'

They pulled their bags out and hurried through the gulf of threatening blackness between the car and the house. Gil's mother forgot her handbag and Gil had to go back for it, then her father didn't believe she had locked the car properly and went to check again, and so it was some minutes before at last they were all inside and Gil was able to take a first long look at her mysterious great-uncle.

Alan Granger was in his sixties but didn't look it. He was very tall, well-built, and had crisply curling hair that had gone grey at the temples while the rest stayed startlingly black. With his great grey bush of a beard, he looked like a demonic Santa Claus. He shook Mr Chandler's hand very gravely, tried to kiss Mrs Chandler, who pulled back and wouldn't let him touch her, then finally looked at Gil.

'Ah, yes,' he said. 'Yes, I see. Gil, isn't it? Your nan's told me a lot about you.'

Gil shook hands, feeling ill at ease. The hall was high-ceilinged and gloomy and the light cast unnerving shadows, especially across Great-Uncle Alan's face. She glanced at the staircase with its carved banisters curving away up into blackness, and shivered.

'How's Biddy?' Great-Uncle Alan asked. 'Any change?'

'No,' Mrs Chandler said sharply. 'And I don't want to talk about it.'

Mr Chandler was frowning at her, clearly baffled by her hostile manner. 'She's no better, but at least she's stable. That's one small mercy . . . but until they've done the tests . . .' He shrugged helplessly.

'Yes . . .' Great-Uncle Alan said. 'Well, come along in.' He ushered them towards a narrow passage that ended in a panelled door. 'Rose has got a meal ready; you must all need it even if you don't feel much like eating.'

Mrs Chandler stopped. 'Rose?'

'She lives with me now. Didn't you know? No, I suppose you wouldn't; it must be, what, twenty years since we last all saw each other? She and Christopher got divorced. It was a bit of a messy business. Leave your bags there, we'll sort them out later.'

Her mouth tightened and she took her handbag from Gil – almost snatched it – and followed Alan Granger along the passage. Gil caught her arm and whispered, 'Mum, is Rose your cousin?'

'Yes. You'd better call her Aunt, I suppose, though she isn't really.'

The door at the end of the passage opened on to an enormous, warm and brightly-lit kitchen. It was cluttered and old-fashioned with a vastly high ceiling, but it felt welcoming after the dismal hall. A smell of burnt potatoes came wafting at them, and someone straightened up from the huge Aga, where she had been taking something out of the oven.

Gil goggled, then felt her face redden and quickly looked away. She hadn't meant to be rude but it was impossible not to stare at Rose. On the whole there was nothing remarkable about her; she was tall and black-haired and slim, like her father. But she wore a piratical black patch over her right eye, and her cheek below the patch was puckered with scar tissue.

'Jean!' Rose put down the dish she was holding, and crossed the floor to envelop Mrs Chandler in a hug. Mrs Chandler didn't flinch away as she had done with her uncle, but she radiated discomfort. 'How many years has it been? I'm so sorry about your poor Biddy! How is she?'

Mrs Chandler mumbled something about having to wait and see, then added, 'I didn't know you were here.' She, like Gil, was trying not to stare too obviously at Rose's face, but suddenly she couldn't stand it any longer and blurted out, 'What *happened*, Rose?'

'Oh, this?' Rose put a hand up to her eye, quite unselfconscious. 'It was years ago. A pan caught fire in the kitchen and the burning fat went in my face. The eye's useless now – cornea gone, or something; I don't know all the medical jargon – and it isn't a very pretty sight, so I use the patch.' Her mouth twitched in a way that wasn't quite humorous. 'It didn't do much for my marriage, either.'

'I'm sorry,' Mrs Chandler said in a frozen little voice.

Rose shrugged. 'I'm used to it; have been for ages. Hardly ever notice the difference now, unless I'm trying to judge distances.'

'Or time.' Great-Uncle Alan had walked to the Aga and was peering uncertainly at the steaming dish on the hotplate.

'Oh – yes, I'm afraid I put the casserole in the hot oven instead of the cool one, so it's a bit overdone. Sorry about that, but I expect most of it'll be all right. Now,' Rose brushed her hands briskly together, 'sit down, all of you. You can tell me all about poor Biddy while we eat.'

Gil was feeling more uneasy by the minute as she sat down with her parents at the great kitchen table. She had known from the start that her mother disliked Alan Granger intensely for some unknown reason, but it was obvious now that for all the talk and surface friendliness her dislike extended to Rose as well. And Rose herself was distinctly strange. She seemed so bright and brisk, yet Gil couldn't shake off the feeling that her manner was an artificial mask hiding something else. The atmosphere at April House felt a little unreal.

Great-Uncle Alan had left the room and now returned. 'I've called Jonas,' he said. 'He'll be down in a moment.'

Mrs Chandler's head whipped round. 'Jonas?' she echoed sharply.

'My son.' Rose looked surprised.

'Oh. Oh, I see. I'd forgotten you had . . .' Her lower lip began to tremble, then suddenly her voice went up shrilly. 'How many more people are you going to spring on us, Alan? Five? Ten?' She choked on the words. 'I only agreed to come here at all because I thought it would be *quiet* – that there'd be no one to *bother* us—'

Mr Chandler said, 'Jean—' and put out a gentling hand,

but she batted it away and started to cry. He looked in embarrassment at Alan and said, 'I'm sorry.'

'No, no, it's all right, Tony. She's under a lot of strain; I quite understand.'

The door opened then. Gil looked round, thankful for a diversion, and met the sharply curious gaze of a tall, lean boy of about her own age, with hair that was exactly the same bright ginger shade.

'Jonas.' Great-Uncle Alan moved quickly from the table, blocking the boy's view of Mrs Chandler. 'This is your cousin Gil. Help her take her bag upstairs to the east gable, so she can get settled in her room.' His glance slid expressively sideways; Gil didn't miss the private signal. 'Now, please.'

Jonas returned his look warily, then nodded and turned back to the door. Gil was only too thankful to leave the kitchen. She simply couldn't cope with Mum in this state, and anything she tried to do would only make matters worse. She got up from the table and trailed out in the red-headed boy's wake.

As soon as they reached the hall and were out of earshot of the kitchen Jonas turned to face her. 'What on earth's going on in there?'

Gil shrugged. 'Mum's a bit upset, that's all. About my sister.'

'Oh, right, of course; my mum told me. I'm sorry.' He paused. 'She said they don't know what's wrong. Is that true?'

Oh God, Gil thought, *I'm beginning to understand how Mum feels. All these questions . . .* 'Look,' she said through clenched teeth, 'I don't really know anything, because Mum and Dad haven't told me, and I don't want to talk about it. It was talking about it that started Mum off again, and if I hear any more, I'm going to start too. OK?' She sniffed, then looked at him half in apology and half in defiance. 'Sorry.'

Jonas nodded. 'OK. I'm sorry, too. I didn't mean to stick my nose in where it wasn't wanted. So let's stop standing here apologising to each other. Which bag's yours?'

'That one. But I'm perfectly capable of—'

He interrupted her, picking the bag up. 'There's a light switch by the stairs, look. Flick it on.'

Gil pressed the switch. Cold light flooded the landing above, and Jonas started up the stairs. She hung back, and he paused. 'Come on, then.'

Suppressing a shudder, Gil climbed after him.

Jonas led her along the landing, then up a second and much shorter flight of stairs that twisted round and ended at two facing doors.

'This is the east gable,' Jonas said. 'Gets all the morning light. Your mum and dad have got the room opposite.'

Gil was secretly relieved that she wouldn't be alone in the gable, though nothing would persuade her to admit it to anyone else. As Jonas reached in to switch on the light she ducked under the low lintel, and looked around in surprise. The room wasn't big but it was very pleasant, cream painted, with a goldy-brown carpet on the floor, goldy-brown curtains with a pattern of pheasants and a matching bedspread. There was a bedside table with a lamp on it, a chest of drawers, and a shelf with some books and ornaments. No radiators – Gil had already guessed from the general chill that the house didn't have central heating – but a small electric blow-heater stood unplugged near the wall socket.

'It's nice,' she said. 'It's really nice.' She went to the shelf and started to look more closely at its contents.

'The books are mine,' Jonas said. 'You might not have read them.'

There were about six paperbacks and two battered old hardbacks. Gil flicked through the paperback titles but they all sounded old-fashioned and were by authors she had never heard of. She tried to sound genuine as she said 'Thanks,' and moved on. Next to the books was a little china unicorn, white with gold hooves and horn and a fake jewel over its heart. Tacky was the word that came to Gil's mind; but on the shelf below was another ornament and this one intrigued her. It was very small, and it was the carved figure of a wizened, gnomelike man with an enormous head, wide eyes and a mischievous grin. The figure was obviously quite old, and the wood from which it was made had been polished to a warm, smooth sheen.

'I like this,' she said to Jonas. 'Is it yours, too?'

'No, Granfa's. He's had him for donkey's years. He's called Touchwood. The idea is, he's made from three different kinds of wood and you touch him for triple good luck – head, heart and feet. Like this.' Jonas tapped the little figure smartly; it rocked backwards and seemed about to fall over, then abruptly righted itself again.

'Clever, isn't it? Whichever way you knock him, he always wobbles back upright.'

The little wooden man's grin was infectious, and for the first time since Biddy's accident Gil found herself smiling, too. Gently she tapped the carving's head, then thought how desperately they all needed some good luck, and suddenly feared she was going to start crying. Not wanting Jonas to see, she turned away and pulled back the curtains over the window. The window was tall and narrow and came to a triangular point at the top; the gable shape, of course. It had small diamond panes and an old-fashioned curly metal catch, and there was a ledge between the glass and curtains.

'There's a good view in daylight,' Jonas told her. 'Over the garden and down towards the dunes. There are trees between here and the sea, but in winter when there aren't any leaves, you can just see the water.'

Gil wasn't really listening. She was looking at the ledge, where someone had placed a shallow bowl filled with an assortment of fresh leaves and dried flowers. Gil hardly knew a pansy from a chrysanthemum, but even she could see that there was something odd about the arrangement. Nothing seemed to fit with anything else in the bowl; as if whoever had put them here had simply scrambled together anything they could find, without any thought for the result.

'What are you looking at?' Jonas asked.

'Oh – just these flowers that someone's put here.'

Jonas peered over her shoulder. For a moment there was silence, then he said, a little tightly, 'Mum did them, I expect . . . Do me a favour, will you, Gil? Don't move them, OK?'

She turned round and stared at him. 'Why not?'

He was looking at her, his green eyes steady, almost hard. 'It'd hurt her feelings.'

He was lying; she knew it, and he knew she did. But however challengingly Gil stared back Jonas wouldn't look away, and at last she was the one who gave in.

'All right.' She shrugged. 'I wasn't going to touch them anyway.' Certainly not now. If there was something funny about those flowers, she wanted to know what it was before she even *looked* at them again.

'Right, well.' Jonas shoved his hands into his jeans pockets. 'I suppose we'd better go downstairs, then. Everything's probably calmed down by now, and dinner'll be waiting.'

Gil nodded, glad to change the subject. She pushed her doubts about the flowers away and followed him towards the door.

3

By the time Gil went to bed that night she was only too glad to get away from everyone else in April House. The room was freezing, so she plugged in the electric fire and left it to warm the air a bit while she went to the bathroom. Then she fished the T-shirt she liked to sleep in from her case, turned the fire off and got into bed.

It had been well past midnight by the time the awful meal had finished. Her father and Aunt Rose had done their best to keep everyone's spirits up, but their efforts had been doomed from the start. Mum had stopped crying but wouldn't talk about Biddy, and to talk about anything else seemed tactless somehow. So they had eaten the burnt casserole, followed by a revolting dessert which smelled like stewed face-flannels, and after that everyone seemed only too thankful to go to bed. Now, with just the glow of the bedside lamp to cheer her, Gil tried to gather her thoughts about her newly discovered relatives. It helped to distract her from worrying about Biddy.

She didn't know what to make of Uncle Alan. He had told her to drop the 'Great' bit, saying it was too much of a mouthful, but though on the surface he seemed so friendly, Gil wasn't entirely sure that he meant it. There was something slightly hollow in the friendliness;

several times, at the edge of her vision she had caught him watching her with a frown on his face, as if she had done something that he didn't want her to. It made her wary.

Jonas was OK. He didn't say a lot, but once or twice he had exchanged a smile with her that suggested he understood exactly how she was feeling, which was more than anyone else seemed to do. Under happier circumstances she thought it would be easy to become good friends with him.

Rose, though . . .

Gil had a weird feeling about Rose. She seemed nice enough – kind, if a bit of a scatterbrain – but she made Gil's flesh creep. Perhaps it was the eye patch, she reasoned, trying to shrug off her sense of unease. Hard to be sure. But something wasn't quite right . . .

A stair creaked outside the room then. Someone was climbing up to the gable. Gil sat up in bed, hoping it was Mum, come to say goodnight. But when the door opened, Rose was standing on the threshold.

Gil's heart thumped and missed a beat painfully. Rose smiled at her and came in, closing the door behind her. 'I thought you'd be asleep.'

'No, I was just . . .' But she didn't finish as an uneasy thought occurred to her. *If Rose thought that, why did she come in?*

'First night in a strange place, I know,' Rose said. 'I thought I'd just make sure you were all right.' She glanced at the window, then at the shelf. 'Jonas showed you Touchwood, I expect.'

'Yes, he did.'

'Good. Good.' She twisted her hands together, almost nervously. 'Right, then. I'll say goodnight.'

'Yes. Goodnight. Thanks.'

Rose pulled the door open again. Then she paused and turned back. 'Gil, I . . . well, you'll think I'm silly, but I – I brought something for you.' She was wearing a plastic apron, and she fished in its large pocket with unsteady fingers. 'It's a little welcome present.'

Out of the pocket came what looked like a crumpled heap of dead leaves. Gil stared at it, baffled.

'It's a necklace,' Rose told her, a faintly desperate edge to her voice. 'I don't suppose you know much about Norfolk, do you, Gil? Round here it's a – a sort of welcome gift – a good luck charm, sort of thing. Traditional.' She came across to the bed and held the object out, almost thrusting it in Gil's face. 'Wear it, Gil. Tonight. For me.' Her expression tightened. 'Please.'

Gil took the necklace from Rose's outstretched hand. *Funniest tradition I've ever heard of*, she thought. And why was Rose so intense about it? As though there were evil spirits all around the house! Still, if it shut her up, Gil thought she might as well go along with it. *Humour her. Why not?*

She forced a smile and said brightly, 'Thanks, Aunt Rose. I'll wear it, of course I will.'

'Good girl.' Rose spoke with relief, and as though Gil were a four-year-old. 'Goodnight, then. Sleep well, love.'

Gil stared at the door for a very long time, half convinced that it would suddenly fly open again and reveal Rose on the threshold brandishing an axe. She was still clutching the 'gift' in one hand, and at last, when she was certain Rose really had gone away, she looked at it. Half-dead leaves and more dried flowers, all tied together with cotton thread to make a crude garland. It stank, too – and something about the haphazard way it had been put together reminded Gil of the bowl on her window ledge.

With a violent movement she flung the necklace away, and scrambled out of bed. There was a waste basket on the other side of the room, lined with a plastic carrier bag. She took the bowl from the ledge and upended its contents into the bag, then snatched the necklace from where it had landed and shoved it in as well. She thumped and squashed the stuff until it was thoroughly crushed, then tied up the bag and pushed it as far down into the bin as it would go. Dead leaves and dried flowers – the whole thing was *insane*!

Gil climbed back into bed and lay shivering under the blankets. She had no intention of turning the lamp off, at least not until she heard her parents coming upstairs and was sure they were close by in the next room. Even then, she doubted if she would sleep.

Please God, she thought fervently. *Please don't let us have to stay here. I want to go home!*

Gil did sleep eventually but badly, a sleep filled with ugly dreams. At last she woke, to find the lamp still on. She'd heard her parents come upstairs and had meant to turn it out. Must have dozed off . . .

She reached out to press the switch – then stopped as she heard the noise.

It was a voice, but it was muffled and indistinct. At first Gil thought it was coming from the room below; someone talking, or the sound of a TV or radio. But as her ears attuned to the direction, she realised that the source was outside. Whoever it was, was whispering in the garden, outside her window.

Gil got out of bed and crossed the floor to the window. At the back of her mind she had a nagging feeling that she shouldn't be doing this. But she *had* to know what was going on.

Pulling the curtain back, she peered into the night.

There was nothing out there. Only the overgrown garden and the silhouettes of trees beyond, dim in the moonlight. The moon also cast shadows in the ivy outside her window, and the shadows were flickering in the night breeze. That was what the noise must have been; wind rustling the ivy, a few strands maybe tapping against the glass. The casement didn't fit properly, either, so that probably rattled. Certainly there was a draught coming in through the gap. Gil reached out, meaning to try to force the window more tightly shut. Then, hand half way to the catch, she stopped.

The ivy *was* rustling; she could hear it, a thin, scratchy, whispering noise. And mingled with the whispering was the other sound, the sound she had first heard. They were not the same.

Gil held her breath, listening intently. Yes, she could separate the two sounds now. The strange one, the unexplained one, was definitely like human voices, flat and hissy, as if below in the dark garden several people were whispering and muttering together. Gil's pulse started to speed up uncomfortably. She tried to pick out words, but the noises were too vague and muffled.

Suddenly they stopped. It took Gil a few moments to realise that they were gone, because the wind in the ivy was confusing and smudged everything. But when she did realise, she frowned and pressed her face to the glass, hands cupped in an effort to block out the lamp's reflection and see better.

Odd . . . There was a shadow on the overgrown lawn that she would have sworn wasn't there before. It seemed to reach out from the tangled wood beyond the garden, tall and gaunt, like a huge finger laid across the grass. It was moving. No, wait; not moving – *growing*. Gil's eyes widened and she tried to tell herself she must be seeing things; it was the moon, clouds, a trick of the light. But in the pit of her stomach she knew better. The shadow *was* growing. It was stretching out, longer and longer, closer and closer; but though she strained her vision to the limit she couldn't see what cast it. Eerily, unnervingly, it seemed to have a life of its own.

Gil's heart tried to climb up into her throat. She wanted to pull away, shut the curtains, run back to bed and not look any more. She couldn't. A power beyond her control was holding her fixed, hands and face pressed to the window. Still the shadow grew longer and nearer, and now it was taking on a distinct shape; a strangely pointed head, curves below the head which might be shoulders . . . It was halfway across the lawn, drawing closer to the house with every moment, and Gil had a sudden wild and terrible feeling that it was searching for something.

Then she realised: the shadow *was* searching, and it had found what it wanted. It was reaching across the garden, straight towards the house – straight towards her gable window.

'No . . .' Gil's voice came out as a croaking whisper. 'Oh, no, please . . . this isn't real. It isn't, it *isn't*!'

The thrall that had been holding her snapped suddenly. She stumbled back, making a wild grab at the curtains and snatching them together to shut it out, shut it *out*! Then she whirled across the room and scrambled into bed, pulling the blankets over her head and clutching the pillow like a long-lost friend. For perhaps ten seconds she huddled there, teeth clenched, eyes screwed shut, and had almost begun to believe that nothing was going to happen—

When with an almighty crash and splintering of glass the window was smashed in from outside, and Gil started to scream the house down.

'There you are, love, see?' Gil's dad shut the curtains and came back to her bed displaying several small pieces of broken glass on his palm. 'Just one of those little diamond panes.' He glanced at Alan Granger. 'It must have been the ivy. Must have tapped on a flaw in the glass. Sheer fluke.'

Gil looked miserably from one to another; her father, her mother and her great-uncle. A minute ago Jonas had put his head round the door to ask what was up, but Alan had frowned severely at him and snapped at him to go back to bed. Rose, thankfully, hadn't appeared. And Gil felt such a complete fool that she could have crawled away and hidden under the carpet.

The explanation, of course, was simple and mundane. She had been half asleep when she went to the window, and in that sort of half-waking state the mind did strange things. The whispering voices, the shadow – she had dreamed them, and she had been trapped in the delusion until the moment when a strong gust of wind had knocked a stray ivy stem against her window. The noise of one tiny pane breaking had crashed into her mind like the end of the world, and she had jerked fully awake

39

in screaming terror. Dad had come running in, Mum at his heels, and Uncle Alan had appeared a minute later. Now Gil was trying to explain and apologise at the same time, while Mr Chandler said never mind, it didn't matter, first night in a strange house and what with everything else it was hardly surprising, and Mrs Chandler smiled pallidly and said she was sorry she had been so horrible all evening. Only Alan seemed uneasy. He had glanced at the waste-basket, clearly noticing the leaves bagged up and dumped in it, and now he kept looking sidelong at the window. But he agreed aloud about the ivy, and asked Gil if she would like a hot drink to help her get back to sleep. Gil said no, thank you, she'd be all right now, and she was really sorry to have been such a nuisance to everyone.

'I'll get the window seen to in the morning,' her uncle promised. 'These curtains should be thick enough to keep the draught out tonight, but if you get cold, Gil, just switch on the fire.'

She nodded. 'Yes, I will. Thanks, Uncle Alan . . . and sorry.'

'No harm done; that's what matters.' He smiled at her. The smile was meant to be reassuring, but it didn't quite work. 'Goodnight. Sweeter dreams this time, eh?'

He left the room, and Mrs Chandler asked Gil, 'Would you like me to stay with you for a bit, till you go back to sleep?'

Truthfully, Gil would have liked company, but she also felt it wouldn't be fair to ask. 'No, Mum,' she said, 'I'm fine, honestly. You and Dad go back to bed.'

'Well, if you're sure.' She stood up. 'But if you want anything, we're just across the passage.' She bent suddenly, impulsively, to kiss Gil; something she hadn't done for quite a long time. 'Night, night. And don't worry – there's nothing to be frightened of.'

When her parents had gone, Gil thought about her mum's last remark. Of course there was nothing to be frightened of. She'd had a bad dream, that was all. Rummaging in her bag, she found her personal stereo and tuned it to a local commercial station that was playing late-night rock. She wasn't going to think about dead leaves or shadows or breaking window-panes. A little music, and maybe one of Jonas's books, however boring, to keep unpleasant thoughts at bay. She'd be all right.

For tonight, anyway.

4

There was what Nan would have called 'an atmosphere' in the kitchen when Gil walked in the following morning. Everyone except Jonas was there and they were all trying to behave naturally, but it was obvious that they had been arguing. Mrs Chandler's face was pinched and pale and angry, Mr Chandler was staring at the wall and looking embarrassed, and Rose was making a lot of unnecessary clatter and fuss by the Aga. Only Alan seemed calm, but there was a stubborn look in his eyes.

Gil sat down on an empty chair and Rose came over to the table like an anxious mother hen.

'You must have *something*, Jean, even if it's only toast,' she said to Gil's mother. 'You can't go all day on an empty stomach, and as you won't be going to the hospital straight away—'

'Won't be going to the hospital?' Gil's voice climbed up half an octave in alarm. 'Why? What's happened?'

'It's all right, love.' Mr Chandler reached across the table and patted her arm. 'We've phoned them, and there isn't any change in Biddy. But they've done all the tests they can with their facilities, and they're still not sure what's wrong.'

'Inconclusive,' Mrs Chandler cut in, in a tight, furious little voice. 'That's what they said. Inconclusive.'

'So you see, Gil, we're not sure what's going to happen now,' he went on. 'They might move Biddy to London. They'll make the decision when the consultant's seen her later this morning, and then they'll phone us here. That's what we're all waiting for.'

Gil's stomach felt ice-cold. 'Inconclusive' was another way of saying that the doctors still had no idea what was wrong with Biddy. That was crazy! How could they not know by now? How many different tests *were* there, to find out what could make a healthy kid keel over unconscious?

Clutching at straws, she said desperately, 'Could it have been a snakebite or something? There might be adders—'

Her mother exploded before she could finish. 'Don't be so *stupid*, Gil! For God's sake, don't you think they've *thought* of everything like that?'

'All right, Jean, all right. Gil's only trying to help; no need to flare up at her.'

Mrs Chandler sniffed, wiped her nose and nodded. 'Yes. Yes, all right. Sorry, Gil, I didn't mean . . .' She waved a hand, unable to finish.

Rose came to the table bearing laden plates. 'Try and eat,' she pleaded again. 'It *will* do you good, Jean, if you can just try.'

Stony silence answered her. Rose sighed, put the plates down and went to the door to call Jonas.

★ ★ ★

The breakfast consisted of everything that Gil knew was unhealthy: bacon, fried eggs, mushrooms, and something that Rose said was called Colcannon but looked and smelled more like sludge omelette. It all tasted vile, too; the bacon flabby and underdone, the eggs burnt black on their undersides and the mushrooms reduced to chewy little pellets from overcooking. Gil and her mother didn't manage more than a mouthful apiece; Mr Chandler did his best but with a guilty eye on Mum. Only Alan and Jonas ate heartily, though Jonas did give Gil a couple of wry looks. Rose didn't seem to be having anything at all, although she swallowed a cup of scalding tea the colour of old bricks, which the Chandlers all refused.

Jonas disappeared upstairs as soon as the disastrous meal was over, and no one else had anything to say. They were all listening for the phone, and the tension grew and grew, until Gil couldn't bear it any longer.

'Can I go to my room?' she asked.

'Of course,' said Rose. 'Why don't you have a nap? You probably didn't get much sleep last night.'

Gil nodded. The others were all silent as she left the kitchen, and the silence seemed to follow her to the hall. At the foot of the stairs she hesitated, looking up into the gloom of the stairwell. She didn't want to go back to the east gable; it had only been an excuse to get away from the atmosphere round the breakfast table. She would rather be outside in the fresh air, well away from everyone. So instead she slipped out of the front door and into the garden.

There wasn't much to see in the garden, even if she had been interested in plants to begin with. It was little more than a tangle of shrubs that had been left to riot to their hearts' content. A few splashily bright yellow and orange flowers – marigolds, she knew that much – poked up here and there, but apart from that the garden was just an unbroken swathe of dull green. At the far end was a messy, overgrown hedge, with a small wrought-iron gate half off its hinges and nearly buried in the untidy mess. For the sake of something to do Gil mooched towards it; as she approached, a white cat emerged from the hedge, stopped and looked at her.

'Hi, puss.' Gil held out a friendly hand. But the cat only twitched its tail contemptuously and vanished back into the hedge again. *It's that sort of day*, Gil thought. She looked over the rickety gate, hoping there might be something interesting beyond it. There wasn't. Just a narrow, tarmaced road which led away to left and right, with pine trees on the other side. There was no traffic, not even a distant sound of it; in fact everything was oppressively quiet.

So quiet that the distant sound of raised voices from the house reached Gil's ears.

She swung round, her first thought that the hospital must have phoned and there was news of Biddy. At once she started to run back towards the house's brooding grey bulk. The voices sounded as if they were coming from the kitchen; Gil headed for the back door—

Then abruptly halted as she heard what was going on.

'And I said *no*, Alan!' It was her mother's voice, furious, nearly hysterical. 'It's rubbish, and I don't believe it, and I never have!'

'Then you're a fool!' That was Uncle Alan. 'Face the truth, Jean, for once in your life! You should have known better than to bring them anywhere near Neapham in the first place!'

'Don't be ridiculous! I'll do what I like with my own children! And as for this insane suggestion of yours—'

Rose chimed in at that point, trying to make peace, and Gil's dad added his own pleas. The next part of the row was lost in the confusion of voices, and Gil felt a huge wave of misery wash over her. Biddy in hospital, and no one knew what was wrong, and all her mother and uncle could do was argue! She wanted to burst in at the door and scream at them to stop it, *stop* it. But before she could, Alan's voice suddenly came through clearly again.

'Why do you think I've never invited you all here in all these years? Even before I met Gil last night, I saw photographs – they've both got the sign!'

Gil froze, mouth open, ears straining. What was he *talking* about?

46

'Well, so has Jonas!' her mother snarled back. 'If you believe in this tripe, why did you let *him* come and live here?'

'I didn't have any choice! Where else could he and Rose have gone?'

Mrs Chandler's reply was lost amid more peace-making efforts from Rose and Dad. Heart pounding, Gil edged to the kitchen window and pressed herself against the wall, where she should be invisible from inside. Then in the jumble of words she heard Alan say something about 'protection'. Whatever he meant, it made matters worse, for Mrs Chandler stormed back at him.

'*Protection?* This is total nonsense and I'm not listening to any more of it! When we leave, Gil comes with us!'

'All right. It's your choice, and I can't force you to change your mind. But what if you're wrong, Jean? What if it's true?' His voice became grim, almost threatening. 'If Biddy dies, you'll never know, will you? And you'll spend the rest of your life wondering!'

A pulse of shock went through Gil. *If Biddy dies?* She couldn't control herself; she raced for the door and burst in.

'What's happened to Biddy?' Her voice went shrilly up the scale. 'Something has! Tell me!'

They had all whipped round at her arrival, but Mrs Chandler immediately turned her face away again. Alan glared at Gil as though she were an alien invader, while Dad just stared down at the table.

It was Rose who finally reacted.

'It's all right, love,' she said, hurrying to where Gil stood trembling on the doorstep. 'Nothing's happened, as far as we know. We're still waiting for the hospital to ring.'

'But I heard—' Gil stopped as she realised that she didn't want them to know that she had overheard the quarrel. She couldn't explain her reasoning, but it seemed important that they should not find out.

'I heard voices,' she managed to finish. 'I thought someone was calling me. I thought there must be news.'

Mum said, 'Well, there isn't,' in a tight, tense voice, and no one else spoke.

'We'll shout for you when they ring,' Rose assured her at last. She forced a smile. 'Were you in the garden? It's quite a nice morning. Why don't you stay out there for a while, and have a good look around?'

Mrs Chandler tensed as if she was going to snap at Rose, but changed her mind. Alan had shoved both hands in his pockets and was staring out of the window, and Gil's father just went on looking at the table.

'Right,' said Gil in a small voice. 'I might as well, mightn't I?'

She turned. Rose called after her, 'We *will* call you. Promise!' but she didn't respond, just walked away from the house.

Gil went back to the far end of the garden. She guessed that Mum and Uncle Alan wouldn't start arguing again if they thought she might be in earshot, but even if they didn't worry about her and went at each other hammer and tongs again, right now she didn't want to know. The little she had heard was more than enough, and she was starting to think that everyone around her was either mad or heading for it.

She had reached the half-buried gate again and stood staring at it. She wanted to walk through it and away down the road – it didn't matter where; just somewhere as far from April House as possible. But what if the hospital rang, and she wasn't here? Not knowing whether she wanted to stay or go, Gil was dithering when a soft, almost furtive rustling made her swing round.

Jonas had come up behind her, so quietly that he was only two paces away when she heard him. He stopped; Gil backed a step but came up against the gate.

'Hi,' Jonas said.

'Hi.' She watched him warily.

'Sorry, I didn't mean to make you jump.' He paused. 'I heard Granfa and your mum arguing.'

Gil shrugged. She didn't want to discuss it with anyone, let alone with Jonas, who was, so to speak, in the enemy camp. But Jonas wasn't willing to let it go.

'You heard them, too, didn't you?' he persisted.

'What if I did?' Gil countered. 'Arguments happen. It was just one of those things.'

'And what about the row last night? Was that one of those things, too?'

'Last night . . . ?' Gil's face blanked, and a thin, humourless smile twisted Jonas's mouth.

'Ah.' He came towards her, past her, and leaned on the gate, staring out at the road. 'You didn't hear it, then? No; you'd probably gone to sleep by then. They must have had a window open, because the noise carried up to my room. I couldn't make out what they were saying, so I went downstairs and listened.' He said this quite shamelessly, and despite her wariness Gil felt a stirring of curiosity – and disquiet.

'What were they rowing about?' she asked.

'Same thing as this morning,' said Jonas.

He was being deliberately cryptic, Gil thought, and her anger rose abruptly. 'Well, thanks for telling me nothing!' Her voice started to rise, too. 'All *I* heard was a lot of rubbish about signs, and why we shouldn't have come here, and what happens if Biddy – if she—' She choked and gasped, fighting back tears. 'It was rubbish, just *rubbish*!'

Jonas didn't say anything for a few moments. Then: 'Look, Gil . . . can we talk about that?'

'What's the point?' Gil wiped her eyes and glared at him. 'There's nothing to say, is there?'

'I think there is. But I don't want to say it here. Let's go somewhere.' To her surprise he took hold of her arm. 'I know you're worried about the hospital, but whether they ring or not, there's nothing you can actually do.'

His eyes were very intense. Gil said sharply, 'You're hurting my arm,' and jerked herself free. 'If this is some sort of wind-up—'

'It isn't. It's serious. Please, Gil.'

There was a long pause. Gil couldn't imagine what Jonas could possibly have to say that would interest her, or be of any use. But he had at least had the decency to say 'please'. And the uneasy curiosity was creeping back.

'All right.' She nodded once, curtly. 'I'll come.'

Jonas wrestled the gate partly open, they went through and he turned left along the lane. They walked some way without speaking. Gil began to wonder again if, after all, he was playing some sort of joke on her, but pride stopped her from challenging him. Then, at last, he broke the silence.

'It looks as if Biddy might be moved to London.'

The lane was too narrow to walk safely two abreast, so he had twisted his head round to talk over his shoulder. Gil studied the pine trees, not wanting to meet his eye. 'I know,' she said. 'They told me.'

'Well if she is, your mum and dad will go back home of course. I mean, you don't live far from London, do you? So they'll go. But Granfa wants *you* to stay. That's what the row was about.'

Now Gil did stare at him, and an echo of her mother's words came back. *When we leave, Gil comes with us . . .* She swallowed. 'Why? Why on earth should he want that? He told Mum we shouldn't even have—'

'Come near Neapham in the first place; yeah, you said before. I don't know the answer. But now you *are* here, Granfa wants you to stay. He said something like, "the damage is done now and we can't change it".'

'What does *that* mean, for God's sake?'

'I don't know,' said Jonas again. 'I only know what I heard him say last night.' He hesitated, and she had the impression he was weighing something up in his mind. Then: 'He said something else. One particular thing; it stuck in my mind. He said: "You should have kept them well away, because they've both got the sign." '

Gil stopped dead. 'Sign . . .?'

He stopped too, and sighed. 'I know it sounds nuts, but I'm only telling you—'

'Don't bother to explain,' Gil said through clenched teeth. 'It sounds nuts, all right. It sounds completely barking. But I believe you, because I heard him say it, too, this morning.'

Jonas looked down at the road, and Gil was surprised to see the look of relief on his face. Or was there something else? Just now, his voice had sounded . . . desperate? No, that wasn't quite the right word. She had a better one. *Frightened*.

She swallowed. 'Look,' she said, trying to sound calm and reasonable, 'this "sign" thing that Biddy and I are supposed to have. What's it all about, do you know?'

Jonas shook his head. 'Not for certain.'

'But you've got an idea?'

'Well . . .' Jonas eyed her unhappily. 'I think . . . I think maybe it's got something to do with the colour of your hair.'

'Our *hair*?' Gil echoed. This was getting ridiculous! She had already reached the conclusion that Aunt Rose was out of her mind; now it was starting to look as though Uncle Alan was just as crazy. 'OK, so our hair's red – so what? Hell, you've got red hair, too, so if that's your granddad's precious sign, you're stuck with it as well!'

Jonas kicked at a tussock of grass at the roadside. 'Yeah' he said. 'I am, aren't I?' He laughed shortly. 'I'm not sure about the sign; whether it is red hair or not. But there was something that happened years ago, when Mum and I first came to live with Granfa.'

'What?'

'Not here.' Jonas cast a quick look over his shoulder, as if he wanted to reassure himself that the road really was as deserted as it seemed. 'Just a bit further on; then I'll tell you. Come on.' He didn't wait for an answer but set off once more at a rapid pace. Gil held back for a moment. Then she followed.

Jonas walked so fast along the lane that Gil sometimes almost had to run to keep up with him. Neither of them had breath for talking, until Gil saw that the land to their right was changing. Through the belt of pines she could see scrub and marram grass, and beyond that were sand dunes. It looked horribly familiar, and a picture flashed across Gil's mind of Biddy lying still and silent on the sand. This was the same place, or very near it . . . Gil didn't want to go there, and was opening her mouth to say so to Jonas when to her relief he turned off down a smaller, unmade lane that led away to the left. She hurried after him, glad to be veering away from the dunes, and the pines petered out before – some thirty metres on – they came to the end of the lane. Here was a lych gate, and beside the gate a wooden notice board with gold lettering on it proclaimed: 'Parish Church of St. Osyth'.

Jonas was already going through the gate. Mystified, Gil went after him, and he led her towards the church.

It was a pleasant looking building, quite small and modest, built of stone and with a square, squat tower. The churchyard was well tended, the grass short and the graves neat, with flowerbeds between them. The last of the pines flanked it on one side, but Gil was too busy wondering why Jonas had brought her here to look beyond them.

The church wasn't locked, and the door opened with a soft, heavy sound. As they stepped into the cool interior, Gil peered around uncertainly. Apart from weddings and christenings and (sometimes) Christmas, she hardly ever set foot in churches. Her mother liked looking round historic ones, but Gil had never been interested, and she felt uncomfortable and vaguely guilty, as if she had no business being here.

The inside was as pleasant as the outside, with a small altar, rows of old pews instead of modern chairs, and some fine stained-glass windows that softened the gloom and gave it a warm glow. Jonas walked round the font (which was stone, and looked extremely old) and sat down on the end of a back pew, moving up to make room for Gil.

'OK,' he said. 'Nothing's going to disturb us here. Now I'll tell you what happened years ago.'

Gil wondered why he had said 'nothing' rather than 'no one'. But she pushed the thought away and tried not to feel intimidated by the church's echoing acoustics as Jonas continued.

'After my parents got divorced, Mum and I came to live with Granfa. I was only six or seven, and I'd never seen Granfa before – my dad didn't like him, and he'd never been to visit us.'

'Or invited you to him?'

'Right; like he's never invited your people, either.' Jonas laughed shortly. 'He scared the daylights out of me the first time I met him.'

'I can believe it,' Gil said with feeling. 'He looks so . . . forbidding.'

'Oh, it wasn't that,' said Jonas. 'It was the way he reacted when he saw me. He was horrified. He turned on my mum, and asked what the hell she thought she was doing, bringing me here, when I had *that*.'

'Had what?'

'I'm not completely sure, now. But I've got this memory stuck in my mind that he meant my red hair, and that was what horrified him.' Jonas shrugged. 'You know how it is when you're a little kid: you get a daft idea fixed in your head and you stick to it, even if it doesn't make any sense. But I had an incredibly strong feeling that Granfa was scared.'

'*Scared?*' Gil couldn't imagine Alan Granger being scared by anything.

Jonas shrugged. 'Sounds crazy, I know. But Granfa and Mum had a stand-up row about it, right there in the hall, in front of me. Granfa shouted that Mum should have known better than to bring a red-haired child to Neapham, and Mum yelled back that we didn't have anywhere else to go, so what was she expected to do? Then she said something about . . .' He paused, recalling. 'Yes . . . she said, seeing as he knew all about it, and was so good at lecturing people about protecting themselves, why couldn't he protect me?'

'How did your granddad react to that?' Gil asked.

'I don't know. They both suddenly realised that I was standing there gawping and listening, and they shut up. Granfa picked up our cases and took them upstairs, and said he'd talk to Mum later, in private.' Jonas scratched with one fingernail at a dent in the pew in front of them. 'I don't know what they said later, but Mum and I stayed, and neither of them said another word to me about it.'

'Didn't you *ask*? I would have done!'

'Oh, sure. But Mum just said it was a silly misunderstanding between her and Granfa, and nothing to worry about. She never talked about it again.'

'So after that, everything was . . . normal?'

'Yeah. Oh, except for one thing.' Jonas fished inside his sweatshirt and pulled out something that hung on a thong around his neck. 'That first night, when I was in bed, Granfa came up to say goodnight. He gave me this, and he told me to wear it, and never take it off.' He laughed, embarrassed. 'He was so intense about it, he really frightened me, so I did what he asked. I didn't *dare* take it off.'

A small, flat leather pouch was fastened to the thong. Gil looked closely at it, curious. 'And . . . you've worn it ever since?'

Jonas nodded. 'By the time I stopped being scared of what would happen if I didn't, I was sort of used to it; like a habit. Anyway, it keeps Granfa happy.'

Gil pressed the pouch experimentally. There was something loose and brittle inside, that crackled faintly. 'What is it?' she asked.

He shrugged again. 'Dried herbs. That's what Granfa told me, anyway.'

An image of Rose's dead-flower garland formed in Gil's mind, and with it a disturbing thought. *I threw that garland away. I threw away the leaves in the bowl on the window ledge. And afterwards, I saw the shadow in the garden . . .*

57

She pushed the spiralling alarm out of her mind, telling herself not to be so stupid. The dried leaves didn't have any meaning. The shadow had only been a dream. Alan and Rose were just eccentric, believing in some far-fetched superstition that any sensible person would laugh at.

Or on the other hand, they could be playing some twisted game of their own . . .

The unprompted thought shocked Gil, and she glanced quickly at Jonas's throat again. Did he believe in Uncle Alan's mysterious 'sign'? She wanted to ask him outright. But she didn't have the courage . . . because another thought was creeping into her mind on the heels of the first. If Alan and Rose *were* hatching some weird scheme, a small inner voice whispered, then Jonas was as much their victim as she was.

And as she looked at his face, a gut instinct told her that he knew it.

5

'Mum, you don't mean it!' Gil said in horror. 'You don't! Dad—' She looked wildly from one to the other of them. 'You can't leave me behind!'

'Stop it, Gil! I'm not listening to you any more!' Mum turned away so that Gil couldn't see her face. 'You're staying here, and that's all there is to it!' She put a hand up to her face and her voice cracked. 'As if I hadn't got enough to deal with, and you have to—'

'All right, Jean, all right.' Dad reached out and touched Gil's shoulder. 'Gil, love, I know it's not what you want, it's not what any of us wants; but we're only trying to do the best thing we can. Mum and I need to be with Biddy in London, don't we?'

'Yes, but—'

'We can't all three of us stay there; it wouldn't be fair and it wouldn't be right. And you can't possibly live at home on your own.'

'I can!' Gil pleaded. 'I'm old enough to look after myself!'

'Even if you are, think how Mum would feel. She'd be worrying about you the whole time and, like she says, she's already got enough to deal with.' He squeezed her shoulder gently. 'Come on, love. It won't be for long.

And Alan and Rose are family; they'll look after you. Do what we ask. For Mum's sake. And Biddy's.'

The worst thing was, Gil knew she couldn't argue. Dad was so reasonable, trying so hard to be fair. And though Mum was acting like an alien, it was only because of her fear for Biddy. Their decision made sense to them, she could see that.

But she was sure that Uncle Alan had had a hand in it somewhere. And she did not, *did not* want to stay on at April House.

Mrs Chandler said suddenly, 'Well, if you two are going to stand around wasting time, I'm going to get our bags,' and all but ran out of the kitchen. Gil stared after her, face stricken.

'She doesn't mean it, love,' said her dad kindly. 'She's upset and little wonder. But she loves you very much. We both do.'

His own face looked tired and strained, and Gil realised that he was carrying more than his fair share of the burden. She swallowed something that was trying to stick in her throat, and nodded.

'I know. Sorry, Dad.'

'No need for sorry,' he reassured. 'You're worried, too, and scared. I understand. But Alan and Rose will look after you. And there's Jonas; you get on fine with him, don't you?' Gil nodded again. 'Good. We'll phone every day, and the moment there's any news you'll be first to hear it.'

'Yes . . .' Gil sniffed.

'All right, then.' He put on a bracing front. 'Don't you worry. Once Biddy's in the London hospital they'll soon find out what's wrong, and put it right. I bet we'll all be back together again in just a few days!'

'OK,' said Gil. 'Thanks, Dad . . .'

'That's my good girl.' He hadn't called her that since she was little, and it was all Gil could do not to burst into tears. For his sake, she didn't. Instead she forced a watery smile and said, 'Shall I make you and Mum a coffee?'

Mr and Mrs Chandler left an hour later. From the doorstep of April House Gil watched the car dwindle down the track. She still wouldn't let herself cry. Alan and Rose were standing beside her, waving, and she didn't want them to see how upset she was. It would make her feel too vulnerable. And she was already feeling more vulnerable than she had ever done in her life. *Why did they have to leave me behind?* she thought despondently. *Why did the people from the hospital have to ring and say Biddy's going to London? Why did any of this have to happen at all?*

The car had disappeared and she couldn't even hear the distant engine now. Alan and Rose turned away; Rose hesitated and might have said something to Gil, but Alan touched her arm and shook his head. They went inside. Gil waited until she was sure they were both out of the way, then she closed the door, crossed the hall and ran upstairs. She couldn't bear the thought of talking to anyone, even being in the same room as anyone; she only wanted to hide away and be on her own.

Up the second, shorter flight of stairs to the east gable. Gil opened her bedroom door – and saw the bowl, and its contents, on the window ledge.

It was the same collection of dried leaves and twigs, again not arranged in any sort of order but pushed apparently at random into the bowl. Just like last night. Rose, it seemed, wasn't going to take no for an answer.

For maybe five seconds Gil stood staring at the bowl, while a tidal wave of misery and confusion and fear grew inside her. Then she slammed the door shut again, turned to run back downstairs – and came face to face with Jonas on the landing.

'What do you want?' She flung the words at him furiously. 'Why were you creeping up on me?'

'Sorry!' Jonas backed a pace, surprised by the vehemence of her reaction. 'I wasn't creeping, and I didn't mean to scare you. I saw you come up here, and I just thought . . .'

'Thought *what*?'

'That you might want to . . . talk, or something.'

Gil's heart was still pounding with the shock of the unexpected encounter. She didn't believe him, didn't trust him, didn't trust anyone in this hateful house. 'Well, I don't!' she snapped savagely. 'I just want to be left alone!' Pushing roughly past him she started back to the stairs, then stopped and looked back. 'And you can tell your mother that I'm not sleeping in that room while those *things* are still there!'

She stormed away, nearly lost her footing on the first step, regained her balance and vanished downstairs. Jonas didn't follow her. Instead he stood motionless for a few moments.

Then, quietly, he opened the door of Gil's room and went in.

Gil didn't know where she was going, and didn't care. Her eyes and throat were hot with tears; she was trying to fight them back but she was losing the battle, and they came spilling, blurring the lane and the trees ahead of her as she ran. No one had followed her from April House, but she kept running none the less, because running was the only thing that helped.

Two cars passed her on the road, but she wasn't even aware of them. Nor, some minutes later, did she realise that the tarmac under her feet had given way to sand. But when the sand became looser and softer, and running was suddenly a slog that made the muscles in her legs start to ache fierily, she finally slowed down and halted. Reality came back slowly as she stood doubled over and panting, until at last breathing became easier and she raised her head.

When she realised where she was, it was like being punched in the stomach. She was among the sand dunes, with scrubby pines to one side of her and the endless reach of the beach and the sea to the other. Some cynical twist of chance, coincidence, whatever, had led her straight back to the place where she had found Biddy lying unconscious.

Gil straightened her back and stared around. This was the same place, she was sure of it. The way those three trees grew so close together, with their trunks oddly twisted: she'd seen them before. And that nearest groyne was the last one she and Biddy had jumped; she remembered, because part of it was broken and the jump had been easier than all the others. There was a visible path in the sand, leading from the trees and the road. She must have turned off there, without being aware of what she was doing.

The sound of the sea was steady and unchanging, and a sharp little wind snatched at Gil's short hair and blew it stingingly around her face. It wasn't really cold, but all the same she shivered. This was the last place on earth where she wanted to be. Even the prospect of returning to April House was better than staying here, and she turned quickly back towards the path.

Then stopped as a flicker movement between two dunes caught her eye.

She only glimpsed it for an instant, but she was sure it was a person. A small person – and something about them seemed familiar. Suddenly her mouth felt dry, and she called out.

'Hello! Who's that?'

There was no answer. Gil stood for a few moments, watching and listening, then decided that she must have imagined it. Hardly surprising, considering the state she was in; easy to—

The thought broke off as, in the distance, the figure emerged again from behind a dune.

Gil stared, while her brain whirled with a mixture of shock and disbelief. A small girl, her hair as red as Gil's own . . . *It isn't possible*, she told herself. *It isn't, it can't be*—

But it was.

Gil screamed, '*Biddy!*' And the child sprinted away.

'*Wait!*' Gil's voice climbed to a shriek, and she took off after the girl. A part of her knew that the child couldn't possibly be Biddy, but she didn't stop to think things out rationally. The girl was there, and she looked like Biddy; that was all that mattered.

The girl had a head start on Gil, and she knew the territory far better. She dodged among and between the dunes; several times Gil thought she had lost her, only to see her appear again, heading in a zigzag towards the lane. Though the soft sand hampered her, Gil was the faster runner, and she was gaining when the girl reached the wire fence that separated the beach from the road. But the girl was small enough to go straight through the fence, between two strands, and by the time Gil had scrambled through after her she was well behind again.

Gasping and hopping as she straightened up on the other side of the fence, she peered around.

And was just in time to see the child run across the lane and disappear among the further belt of trees.

Gil ran down the bank, just remembered to check for cars, and raced after her. She could see the bulk of a stone tower behind the pines, and realised that it must be St. Osyth's, where Jonas had taken her this morning. It looked as if the girl was heading for the church; she probably thought it would make a good hiding place. *Well, we'll soon see how good*, Gil thought. She didn't know why it was so important to her, but however determined the child was to hide, she was just as determined to find her.

She decided that she must be approaching St. Osyth's from a different direction than before, because the belt of trees seemed denser and there was no sign of the track leading up to the lych gate. It was gloomy among the pines, and hard to make out the shape of the church, until abruptly the trees ended and she stepped out into open ground.

The church was directly in front of her. It was the same size as St. Osyth's, made of the same stone and built to the same design. But it was a desolate ruin.

For one mad moment Gil almost believed that this was the same building she and Jonas had entered this morning, but in just a few hours some terrible catastrophe had crumbled and collapsed it. Then the feeling fled as reason told her it simply wasn't possible. The broken tower of this church was covered in ivy, and the grass in the churchyard was thigh-high and choked with thistles and briars that completely covered the gravestones. This place had been abandoned for *centuries*.

Slowly, she moved towards it. A stone wall had surrounded it once, but many of the stones had fallen and there were gaps that anyone could walk straight through. Off to the left were the remains of a lych gate – again, it looked identical to the one at St. Osyth's – but Gil's gaze was fixed on the derelict church. It had no roof, and the empty windows gaped like unseeing eyes, giving it the look of a huge, strange, dead animal. There was no path that she could find, but she forged through the long grass until she reached the doorway. The door itself was long gone; all that remained was the ancient stone arch, with a floor of broken, moss-covered tiles beneath.

Gil moved under the arch—

And stopped.

It was only a momentary sensation, gone before she could analyse it, but it was as if a warning voice inside her had said clearly: *No.* Gil shook her head and pushed down a shiver. Nerves, that was all. It was natural to be cautious; the ruin's crumbling walls and unstable beams and rubble-strewn floor could be dangerous. But the girl had come in here, she was sure of it . . .

The warning voice had quietened as Gil advanced slowly into the ruined church. Fallen stones shifted and rocked under her feet, and the open rafters overhead looked as if the slightest disturbance could bring them crashing down. There was a dank smell, and shadows reached out from the jagged walls, in which more archways were half hidden. Towards the far end were several long pieces of rotting wood that might once have been pews or a choir stall, and beyond them stood a huge slab of stone that looked like the remains of the altar.

There was no sign of the girl and, when Gil paused to listen, no telltale sounds of anyone moving furtively around. In fact, she realised, there were no sounds at all, not even birdsong. Everything was so *still*; a sort of old, grim, unnatural stillness that sent unpleasant little sensations crawling over her skin. She wasn't exactly afraid, but she didn't want to stay here for longer than she had to. Maybe the girl hadn't come in here after all? Maybe she had dodged round the side of the building, or even doubled back towards the lane and the beach? Gil decided to take one quick look on the far side, where the shadows were denser, and then she was going to get out of this creepy place.

There wasn't so much rubble on the other side of the church, and she could see the outlines of the floor's huge, grey flagstones. Some had traces of letters carved into them, and Gil squeamishly avoided treading on them in case they were tombs. There was another arch set into the wall, but fallen beams blocked the way and a rabbit couldn't have got through, let alone the girl. There was nowhere for her to hide. Unless she had climbed up among the rafters – and surely no one could be mad enough to do that – then she simply couldn't have come in here.

Feeling deflated, and chilly now in the dank shadows, Gil turned to go, then noticed something she had been too preoccupied to see before. Another great stone slab, like the altar. But instead of being flat, the top of this one had a shape carved on it. Gil peered more closely. The carving was ancient and weathered and green with lichen, but it was still recognisable as two life-sized human figures, a man and a woman, lying side by side with their hands clasped piously as if praying. Gil's mother had dragged her around enough historic churches when she was little for her to know what this must be: the tomb of someone wealthy, probably the local Lord of the Manor or something, and his wife. The figures were crude and stylised, like a mediaeval painting, and their faces were so badly worn that it was impossible to tell what they might have looked like. All she could see was that the man had long hair with a sort of circlet on his head, while the woman wore a stiff hood that looked a bit like an old-fashioned nun's wimple.

There was some lettering on the side of the slab, and Gil bent to look at it. Most of it was too eroded to be

readable, but she made out '. . . IC IACI . . .' and then
'. . . OBERT ET IOHAN . . .' Latin, probably; that was
what they used in those days. Gil didn't know any Latin
– but suddenly she remembered another snippet from
afternoons dragging round old churches with her mother.
The first words could be 'HIC IACIT', which meant
something like 'Here is', or 'Here lies'. And 'et' was 'and',
wasn't it? Were the other words the names of the lord
and his lady? 'Obert' could be 'Robert' with the first
letter missing. But 'Iohan' . . .

It was then that, for no logical reason, the atmosphere
inside the ruin started to get to Gil. The silence, from
being just a silence, felt ominous, almost threatening, and
the stale, damp chill seemed to be seeping right into her
bones. Suddenly it was all too easy to imagine this place
at night, when the moon turned the shadows to black
ink and made menacing shapes of the broken stones.

*Like the shadow-finger, stretching and lengthening across the
garden towards her window . . .*

The thought came shockingly and unexpectedly, and
cold waves chased each other across Gil's neck. She flung
a glance over her shoulder, half afraid that she would
see the blank stone eyes of the figures on the tomb flick
into life and stare at her. The little red-haired girl was
forgotten. She just wanted to get *out* of here.

She was running by the time she reached the tumbled
stones of the graveyard wall.

6

Gil's parents had rung from the local hospital while she was out, to say that they and the ambulance were about to leave for London. They had promised to ring again once they arrived and Biddy was admitted, and for the rest of the day Gil was as jumpy as a wild animal, constantly alert for the shrill of the phone bell.

Her mind was a turmoil of dark thoughts. She had made a complete idiot of herself with the red-haired girl; obviously she was just some local kid, and when Gil had yelled at her she was frightened and ran away. Hardly surprising. Gil's only excuse, as she saw it, went back to what Jonas had said about red hair being connected with Alan's mysterious 'sign'. In a crazy moment she had thought the girl might know something that might explain it. Now, that idea seemed ludicrous. But at the time, the urge had been powerful enough to make her chase the girl all the way to the ruined church . . .

Gil didn't want to think about the church, but her mind kept catching her out and tugging her back to it. She was certain that, if the building were whole, it would have been almost identical in every way to the present St. Osyth's. So when had the newer church been built – and, more curiously, why? Surely it would have been easier and cheaper to repair the old one, or at least to knock it down completely and rebuild on the same site? Gil recalled the tomb with the carved figures, and the fragments of Latin inscription she had been able to make out. Robert, perhaps, and a woman whose name began with 'Iohan'. Something about them had made her skin creep. And it wasn't only because of the carving's connection with death and burial.

She was aware that Alan could probably have answered her questions; he had lived here all his life and must know a lot about local history. But Gil shrank from the idea of asking him. For one thing, it would mean telling him where she had been, which she did not want to do. And for another, she had a disquieting feeling that he wouldn't have told her the truth.

She had managed largely to avoid Alan, Rose and Jonas all afternoon; in fact, she thought, they were deliberately and tactfully leaving her alone. But there was no excuse to avoid joining them all in the kitchen for the evening meal. Rose fussed over her as she sat down, Jonas gave a sympathetic smile, but Alan only looked at her with a slight frown on his face, as if his thoughts were miles away. Gil returned the look uneasily, then hunched over her plate.

She was struggling with cremated lamb chops, watery mashed potato and overcooked frozen peas when the phone rang. It was her father; Rose handed over the receiver and Gil said, 'Dad—'

'It's all right, love.' He must have heard the strain in her voice. 'Biddy's safe in the hospital, and Mum and I are fine.'

'What do they say about Biddy?' Gil asked.

'It's too early to know anything yet, but we're seeing the consultant tomorrow morning. Fingers crossed, eh?' he paused. 'Are you OK?'

She wanted to answer, *No, I'm not, I hate it here and Alan and Rose give me the creeps, and I want to be with you!* But instead she heard herself say, 'Course, Dad, I'm fine. Aunt Rose and Uncle Alan are being really kind. Don't worry about me.'

He was relieved, his voice showed it, and she was glad she hadn't blurted out the truth. They talked for a minute or so longer, then Dad said, 'Take care, Gil. Love you lots, and Mum does, too,' and hung up.

Gil couldn't face the meal after that; even if Rose had been the best cook in the world she couldn't have eaten a thing. Rose was concerned, but Alan said, 'Let her be; she'll eat when she feels better,' and when Gil said that all she really wanted to do was go to bed and sleep, no one objected.

Gil went to bed, but not to sleep. Too much was going on in her mind, and though she felt desperately tired, she couldn't settle. She tried listening to her personal stereo, but couldn't concentrate on any of the stations she tuned in to, and at length she gave up and lay with her arms folded behind her head, staring at the ceiling and trying not to think at all. But just when it seemed she might settle, back it came again; the chain of thought that nagged and nagged and wouldn't leave her alone. Biddy. The strange, uneasy atmosphere of April House. The argument between her mother and Uncle Alan; talk of 'danger' and 'the sign'. She still didn't know how Alan had managed to persuade her parents to leave her behind. Oh, sure; it was a practical arrangement, as Dad had said when they told her. But Gil didn't believe that was the real reason. There was something else going on. Something that not even Mum would tell her about.

She turned her head and looked at the window ledge. The dried leaves in their bowl had gone. She suspected Jonas had removed them after she'd snapped at him this morning, but she couldn't decide whether to feel grateful to him for doing it, or angry that he had been in her room without her permission. That, of course, brought new worries to her churning mind. She started wondering why the leaves had been put here, and from there it was only a short step to recalling the pouch Jonas wore round his neck, and the weird garland Rose had tried to make her wear, and why Rose had waited until she was in bed before creeping in with it. Then there had been the dream, and the window-pane breaking, and—

Stop it! Gil told herself ferociously. This was getting out of hand; imagination was running away with her, and if she let it go on like this she'd get seriously freaky.

Shut your eyes and make yourself think of something good. Think of . . .

But suddenly she was so tired that she couldn't think about anything. Her eyelids were heavy and there was a prickling soreness behind them. All she wanted was for everything to go away until morning. It would all look different then.

She reached out, switched the lamp off, and was asleep in two minutes.

Gil started awake certain that someone had called her.

'Yes?' She sat up with a flurry, thinking she must be late for breakfast, then belatedly realised that it was still dark and there was no one else in the room. Yet someone *had* called, she was sure she hadn't dreamed it. A soft call, almost a whisper . . .

'Jonas?' For some reason it was the first thought that occurred to her. She slid out of bed, just able to see in the moonlight coming through the window, and padded to the door. Carefully she eased it open.

There was no one there. Gil shook her head muzzily. She must have been dreaming after all . . . Looking at her watch in the dimness she made out the time: three-twenty. Back to sleep, she thought. But first she would find something else to wear in bed; the room was *freezing*. She took a sweater from her case – and as she put it on, she felt a strange sensation, like a silent, insistent tugging inside her mind.

The window. Look out of the window.

She shook her head again, but the sensation didn't go away. *Look out of the window.* Uncertainly Gil moved towards the ledge and her hand hovered by the curtain. She didn't want to look. But the tugging was so strong, impossible to resist . . . With a quick, jerky movement, before her nerve could give way, she yanked the curtain back.

A cloud had drifted over the moon, and at first she saw only a dark grey blur, merging to black patches where the garden was at its most tangled. Then the cloud passed over, and suddenly the garden was drenched in cold light.

On the overgrown lawn stood the little red-haired girl. She seemed to be looking directly up at Gil's window, and as Gil stared in amazement she lifted one hand and beckoned.

Gil was electrified. What on earth was the girl doing at April House? Had she known Gil was here, or was she looking for someone else? What did she *want*? The child beckoned again, urgently this time, and Gil didn't hesitate another moment. Hauling on jeans and sandals, she was out of the room in seconds and feeling her way, as fast as she could, down the stairs. Thankfully, both Alan and Rose slept in another part of the rambling house, and no one heard her as she bumped into things on her way to the kitchen. Fumble with the back door latch – *come on, come on!* – the door opened and Gil raced outside.

As she rounded the corner of the house she thought

for a dismaying moment that the girl had gone. But then there was movement near the old gate in the hedge and the child reappeared. Gil hurried towards her, not daring to call out in case anyone heard, then slowed down and stopped a few metres away.

'Hello . . .' she said uncertainly.

The girl didn't return the greeting. Instead she gave Gil a sidelong, almost sly look, and said, 'Your sister's sick, isn't she?'

She had a heavy accent that Gil assumed was Norfolk. Gil's heart lurched and she said, 'Yes – we don't know what's wrong with her.'

'I do.'

'*What?*'

'I do,' the child repeated. 'And I can help.'

Gil's heart was pounding now. She couldn't believe this; couldn't allow herself to hope. It was all too crazy, too irrational . . . 'How?' she heard herself say in a shaking voice. 'Please – tell me!'

The girl almost, but not quite, smiled at her. 'I can *show* you,' she said. 'But you have to come with me. Come now.' She held out a hand. Gil moved eagerly to take it – then hesitated. Somewhere, common sense was trying to struggle through her shock and confusion, and it told her that this situation was completely insane. A child, hardly older than Biddy, coming to her in the middle of the night and offering help; wanting her to go with her to God alone knew where—

77

'I . . .' She swayed, torn between going towards the girl and backing away. 'I don't think I should . . . I mean, it's night; it's completely dark. In the morning—'

'No!' the girl interrupted. 'Not in the morning – come *now*!' She darted forward, almost a lunge, and snatched hold of Gil's hand. 'Hurry!'

She pulled, hard, unbalancing Gil so that she stumbled with her towards the gate. Then from the direction of the house came a whisper-shout.

'Gil! Is that you?'

The child let Gil's hand go and dodged out of sight among the bushes. Gil swung round. A torch beam, finger-shaded, was bobbing across the garden towards her, and behind it she made out Jonas's face.

'Gil!' He came to a stop. 'What are you doing out here in the middle of the night?'

A huge anger rose in Gil and she flared at him. 'Go away! It's none of your business – who asked you to follow me?'

'No one asked me,' Jonas said reasonably. 'But I was awake, and I heard you going downstairs. I wanted to make sure you were all right. What the hell *are* you doing?'

Gil shook off the hand that he tried to put on her shoulder, and swung towards the hedge again. 'She's gone!' she hissed in dismay. 'No – don't go! Little girl! Where are you? *Please*—'

'What are you talking about?' Jonas demanded. 'There's no one there.'

'There was!' Gil was nearly sobbing by now. 'She came to find me, and now you've frightened her away!'

'Who came to find you?'

'The girl; the little kid – I saw her earlier today! She knows about Biddy, and she said—'

Jonas interrupted sharply. 'What little kid? What did she look like?'

The sudden tension in his voice surprised Gil, and her frustration and fury with him collapsed. 'Look like . . . ? Well . . . about Biddy's age, I suppose. And she's got red hair, as red as ours—'

Jonas glanced quickly at the empty gateway. Then he grabbed Gil's hand and pulled her, far harder than the girl had done. 'Gil, come away! For God's sake – come *away*, let's get *out* of here!'

Gil took one look at his face, and realised he was terrified. Suddenly an answering fear came climbing and scrabbling up in her own mind – she had no idea what it was, where it came from, but the next thing she knew she was running with him, back towards the sanctuary of the house. They piled in at the back door, Jonas flicked the light on, and they both sagged on to chairs at the kitchen table.

Gil was too shaken to speak, but Jonas took two deep breaths and said harshly, 'Gil, there's something I've got to ask you. And maybe tell you, too. It depends if . . .'

'If what?' She found her voice at last. Her hand was aching; the hand the red-haired girl had gripped. The fingers felt *cold*.

Jonas went to the back door and locked it. Then he said, 'Last night – that dream you had.'

She looked at him warily, wondering how much he had been told. 'What about it?'

'*Was* it a dream?'

She didn't answer. Jonas's eyes focused steadily on her. 'Or did something scare you? Something in the garden?'

She shivered so violently that any doubts he might have had instantly vanished – and suddenly she found herself telling him the whole story. The whispering voices mingling with the rustling of the ivy, the shadow lengthening across the grass like a searching finger, and, finally, the shattering window-pane that had set her screaming. When she had finished, Jonas said nothing for some while. Instead, he went to the inner door, eased it open and peered out into the dark hall.

'OK. We haven't woken Mum or Granfa.' He came back to the table and sat down. 'The same thing happened to me.'

Gil tensed. '*When?*'

'Ages ago. I was probably eleven or twelve, the last time. But it was exactly the way you've described it; a muttering voice, then that long, pointed shadow reaching across the garden and coming towards me. The east gable used to be my bedroom, you see. I saw that shadow . . .

80

oh, five, maybe six times. In the end I asked if I could change rooms. I pretended it was because I wanted more space, so Granfa gave me a bigger room on the other side of the house. I haven't seen the shadow since then.'

'So you didn't tell Aunt Rose or Uncle Alan about it?'

He shook his head. 'I've never told anyone before. You see, I convinced myself it didn't really happen, that it was just bad dreams, or a phase; you know the kind of thing. Now, though . . .' He paused. 'Gil, when you saw it, did you see where it came from? Which direction?'

She frowned. 'I think . . . no, I *know*. It came from the bit of woodland at the end of the garden.'

'Not from the gate and the lane?'

She thought again. 'No,' she said. 'It was from the wood. Definitely.'

Jonas nodded. 'Right. That's where it came from when I saw it, too; every time. When I worked it out, I checked where that direction led.' He paused a second time. 'Remember when I took you to St. Osyth's? Well, you don't know this, but there's another St. Osyth's, just—'

Gil said sharply, 'The ruin?'

He was taken aback. 'You *do* know about it?'

'More than that. I've been there.'

'What? When?'

'Today – well, last night. I . . . followed someone there.'

'Who?' But from his expression it was clear that he had already guessed, and the last of Gil's defences went down. She told him how she had left April House, run blindly down the lane and ended up among the sand dunes where she had found Biddy; then about the red-haired child who had fled from her and led her to the ruin.

'You went in?' Jonas sounded worried.

'Yes. But I didn't find her.'

'And she came here tonight?'

Gil nodded. 'Do you know her, Jonas? Do you know who she is?'

'No. But I've seen her. And another one; a boy, a bit older. He's got red hair, too.' Jonas sucked in breath. 'I saw them in several places, around the same time as I kept seeing that shadow.'

'Maybe Uncle Alan would—'

'No.' He interrupted so quickly that she was startled. 'I asked him about them, once; I thought they must be local kids who I didn't know, and I might make friends with them. He said there weren't any other children with red hair around here.'

Gil was astonished. 'But you saw them.'

'Granfa said I must have imagined it.' As Gil tried to make sense of that he added, 'But that's not the main thing. I just said, didn't I, that I wondered if I could make friends with them. Well, think about it. I was nine, maybe ten, at the time. The boy was around the same age, and the girl a bit younger. How old was the girl *you* saw?'

'About Biddy's age,' Gil told him. And then realised what he was getting at. 'My God . . .' Her eyes widened. 'If it *is* the same girl, then . . . she hasn't got any older!'

'And from the way you described her, I'd say the chances of her being someone else are about a million to one,' said Jonas grimly. He stood up, pushing his chair violently back. 'I don't know what we're dealing with, Gil, but there's something seriously weird going on! And I think—' He stopped in mid-sentence, and his hand closed around the leather pouch on its thong, as if it was a talisman. 'When I first came to live here,' he continued, 'Granfa made me promise never to go near the old church. He said it was dangerous. I thought the danger was in the building; that it might collapse on anyone who went scrambling around in there.' He paused, watching Gil carefully. 'OK, fair enough. You've seen the state of it for yourself. But I don't think that's what Granfa really meant. I think there's much, much more to it. And I think Granfa knows what it is.'

A cold, sick feeling had settled in Gil's stomach. 'We've got to talk to him,' she said. 'We've got to get him to tell us!'

Jonas gave a cynical laugh. 'No chance! He'd say we were talking rubbish, then he'd get angry and tell us to shut up about it.' He clenched and unclenched his fists. 'Doesn't take a genius to work it out, does it? Biddy and the sign; the other red-haired kids; the shadow in the garden and the old church – they're *all* tied in somehow. Granfa knows, and our mums do, too, even if they only half believe it. But they don't want *us* to find out the truth.'

'Why?' Gil whispered.

Jonas shrugged. He was angry, she saw; angry and frustrated. 'Maybe they think we'll laugh. Or they think we'd be frightened by it. Or maybe . . .' He looked at her, such an intense look that Gil shrank back. 'Maybe *they're* the ones who are frightened. And that's what they don't want us to realise.'

7

Gil and Jonas went to their rooms soon afterwards, but Gil didn't even attempt to sleep again. She was too shaken by what had happened, and by what Jonas had told her about his own sightings of the red-haired children. Again she had tried to argue that they should tackle Alan; again Jonas had refused . . . and she could see his point. But they had agreed on one thing. This mystery had to be solved. And if no one else would help them, they must solve it alone, once and for all.

The thought that the red-haired girl might come back, and stand staring up at the window without her being aware of it, made Gil's skin crawl. So she sat on the ledge in her gable, gazing past the half-drawn curtain at the dark garden and keeping watch. If the girl did return, she was determined to be ready – but how she would react was another matter. All very well to tell herself that she would rush outside, confront the child and demand answers. It was easy to be brave in theory. Very different, though, when you were actually put to the test . . .

She wasn't tested. The sky turned pearly with dawn, and there had been no sign of the girl. At last Gil stood up, stretching stiff muscles and yawning. She was very tired, but her mind was still too active for sleep. Not six o'clock yet. No one would be up. And there was just enough light to see her way around the garden. Maybe if she went outside and looked, she might find some sort of trace, or clue; anything that might give her a hint in the right direction.

She crept down the stairs and across the hall. A bright bar was showing under the kitchen door and at first she thought that she and Jonas must have left the light on. But when she opened the door, she found that someone else was up before her.

'Hello, Gil!' Rose turned round from the Aga, clearly surprised. 'You're an early bird today. Is everything all right?'

'Oh . . . yes, fine, Aunt Rose.' Gil tried to hide her dismay. 'I – um – woke up and didn't feel like going back to sleep.'

'Well, so long as there's nothing wrong.' Rose smiled kindly. 'I must admit I'm not usually up at this hour myself, but Dad – Uncle Alan – is going off to some conference in Norwich and he wants to make an early start, so I thought I'd make sure he has a good breakfast before he goes.' She waved one hand at a covered pan that was simmering in a sinister sort of way on the hotplate. 'Would you like some? Poached eggs with tomatoes; and there's some toast doing, too – oh, damn!' She grabbed the lid of another hotplate, winced, sucked her fingers and lifted the lid again, with an oven glove this time. There was a billow of black smoke, an acrid smell, and Rose stared sheepishly at the jet-black squares on the plate. 'Well, it'll probably be all right if you scrape the worst bits off . . .'

Gil tried not to cough as the smoke stuck in her throat and said, 'Thanks, Aunt Rose, but I'm not hungry. I'll do myself something later.' She paused. 'Uncle Alan's going to a conference, did you say?'

'Yes. Some organisation of retired doctors, or something; I don't really know.'

'Right.' Hoping she sounded casual, Gil added, 'How long will he be away?'

'Oh, he'll be back this evening. Dad isn't a great one for socialising; he won't want to stay for the dinner or whatever it is they're having afterwards.'

That, then, gave her the whole day. Which could be very useful . . .

She offered to make tea (one way of ensuring it was drinkable) and was mashing bags in the pot when Alan came in, wearing pressed trousers, a sports jacket and a tie. He, too, was surprised to see Gil up and about so early, but he didn't seem suspicious. In fact his mood was unusually cheerful, so Gil decided to risk a leading question.

She said, as if the thought had just slipped idly into her mind, 'Is there a manor house round here, Uncle Alan?'

Rose looked up. Alan regarded Gil thoughtfully. 'No, not any more,' he replied. 'Why do you ask?'

'Oh . . . I thought I saw a big house in the distance, when I went exploring yesterday. I just wondered what it was.'

'Exploring' was Gil's excuse for the outburst that had sent her running from April House, but Alan let it pass. 'No,' he said again. 'It was probably a barn you saw.'

'Oh.' Pause. 'But there was one once, you said?'

She thought Alan hesitated a moment, as if weighing up whether to answer or change the subject. Then he replied carelessly, 'Yes, there was; but it was pulled down well over a hundred years ago. There's just the farm there now.'

Gil nodded. 'Did the family die out?'

'Well, the original family went centuries before that, and it had a number of other owners. The last one was a new-rich Victorian; he'd made his money in iron or coal or something. He started rebuilding the house in the grand Gothic style, but his ideas were bigger than his bank balance, and he went broke.'

Gil started to pour tea. 'So it wasn't him who built the new church, then?'

This time Rose's reaction was more noticeable, but before Gil could look at her she had turned quickly away again. Alan's grey eyes seemed to darken, like clouds before a storm, and he repeated cautiously, 'The *new* church . . . ?'

'Yes,' said Gil innocently. 'St. Osyth's, isn't it called? I had a look inside. I thought it was rather nice.'

He nodded. 'I agree, it is nice – but it's hardly new. It was built in the fifteenth century; long before Victorian times.'

'Oh, right. I thought maybe it was the house owner's idea; you know, to copy the other church, the one that's a ruin now. It was the kind of thing the Victorians did, wasn't it?'

Alan's eyes grew darker still and his voice became sharp. 'You mean, you've seen old St. Osyth's as well? I hope you didn't go in there!'

'No,' Gil lied. 'I just saw it through the trees. That's why I thought the other one must be much newer.'

He relaxed visibly. 'It is much newer. The original was built in the twelve hundreds.'

'Oh,' she said again. 'That's weird.'

'What is?'

For a nerve-racking moment Gil wondered if she had made a major tactical mistake by mentioning the ruin. But if she had blundered, it was too late to back down now. Better to stick to her guns and get to the question she really wanted to ask.

She took a deep breath and said, 'To build another church right next door. Wouldn't it have made more sense to rebuild the first one?'

Alan stared at her so hard that it was all she could do not to flush crimson and drop her own gaze to the floor. The silence lasted for several seconds. Then, to her surprise and relief, he laughed.

'Do you know, I think everyone who comes to Neapham asks that question! But there's nothing sinister about it, Gil; it's perfectly simple. The first church, you see, was built right over an underground spring. No one knew the spring was there, and at first they couldn't work out why the church subsided, and the walls cracked, and the crypt kept flooding. It took them about a hundred and fifty years to find out what the problem was, and then they did the only sensible thing: they abandoned the church and built a new one in a drier place. That's the "mystery", Gil. Nothing more than that.' He reached across the table to refill his teacup. 'And it's why I said I hoped you didn't go into the old church – or anywhere near it for that matter. It's unstable and dangerous; something as ordinary as the vibration of a jet aircraft flying overhead could bring a ton of stone down on you. So stay well clear of it, promise me?'

He was looking at her again with that penetrating, steady look. Gil nodded. 'I promise, Uncle Alan,' she said.

And knew that the story he had just told her was a pack of lies.

Alan left half an hour later, and almost as soon as he had gone Rose said, 'I'm going in to town to do a bit of shopping, Gil. Would you like to come? Or is there anything I can get for you?'

'No, thanks, Aunt Rose.' Gil replied to both questions.

'I'd rather stay here. Mum and Dad said they'd ring this morning.'

'Of course.' Rose smiled sympathetically. 'Well, help yourself to anything you want. I should be back by lunchtime. Oh, and give Jonas a shout if it gets too late, won't you? He'll sleep all day if he gets half the chance!'

That, Gil thought, was very useful information. She stood on the front doorstep as Rose drove away in her old banger of a car (which had enough dents and scratches to suggest that her driving was about as good as her cooking), then looked up at the west gable, where Jonas's bedroom was. The curtains were still firmly closed. Good. She didn't want to go behind Jonas's back. But if he knew what she was planning to do, he might try to stop her – and Gil didn't intend to be stopped.

Back in the kitchen she ate a slice of bread spread with strawberry jam, then went to her great-uncle's study. It was a large room, tucked away from the noisier part of the house and with a large French window that overlooked the garden. The sky was grey this morning, and a sharp east wind was blowing. It rattled the window-panes and made cold draughts in the room; outside, the trees beyond the garden gate were tossing restlessly. Gil switched on a light to relieve the gloom, then stood looking at the rows of bookshelves that lined one wall. Alan had quite a library; a lot of the books were medical ones, but at one end of the shelves there was a collection of big, old volumes on various historical

91

subjects. Her gaze skimmed past *Shipwrecks of the Eastern Coast, The Victorian Philanthropists* and various others, then came to rest on two titles: *The Historic Families of Norfolk* and *Church Architecture Through the Ages*. It seemed too much of a coincidence to find these books side by side, and Gil took them down from the shelves. Great families . . . there had been a grand manor house round here, long ago. And the ruined church contained a tomb that had obviously been made for someone wealthy. Robert, and his wife – presumably – whose name was Iohan–something. She didn't know their surname. But if the church was abandoned before the fifteenth century, as Alan had said, that narrowed the field down a little . . .

She took *Church Architecture Through the Ages* to the window seat and started to leaf through it. The writing was very dense and flowery, and the only photographs seemed to be of countryside scenes or people on horseback. She turned to the index and looked for Norfolk. There was an entry for Neapham, so she turned eagerly to the page.

'The parish church of St. Osyth in Neapham was completed in 1437, and boasts one of the locality's finest examples of . . .' Wait a minute, Gil thought. 1437 – that must be the new church. What about the old one? She read on. But there was no mention of the old church at all.

Strange . . . Gil put the book aside and picked up *The*

Historic Families of Norfolk. This index had quite a few mentions of Neapham; she started to go methodically through the entries but couldn't find a Robert. She was on the fifth reference when, out of the blue, a sudden uneasy feeling nudged at her. A feeling that someone was standing right behind her . . .

Gil's heart gave a huge, painful lurch, then started to beat very fast. She took a deep breath, and her head whipped round.

Jonas was three paces away.

'Oh, God!' Gil shut her eyes in relief. 'Don't *do* that! You gave me such a fright!'

'You weren't supposed to know I was here,' said Jonas. His gaze slid to the book in her hands. 'Not until I'd got close enough to see what you're reading.'

There was no point trying to lie to him, and Gil sighed. 'All right. I'm trying to find out something about the old church, while no one else is around. And the only reason I didn't tell you was because I thought you might not let me come in here.'

Jonas smiled thinly. 'Remember what we said to each other last night? About solving this mystery no matter what?'

She looked away. 'Yeah. I just didn't know whether . . .'

'Whether I meant it? Well, I did.' He shoved his hands into his jeans pockets. 'But I'll tell you one thing; we won't find what we're looking for in any of those books. I know, because I've already tried. There's nothing about the old church in any of them. Nothing at all. And that in itself's weird.'

Gil nodded. 'I thought I might find out something about Robert and his wife,' she said, 'but—'

Jonas interrupted, frowning. 'Who?'

'Robert and – well, I suppose she was his wife. Her name begins with I-O-H but I couldn't read all of it; it was too—'

'Wait a minute. What are you talking about?'

Gil realised suddenly that, though she had admitted she had been inside the ruined church, she hadn't told him about the tomb. She hesitated, not sure whether to tell him now, not sure of anything, and they continued to look at each other for a few seconds. Then Jonas said, 'You've got a straight choice, Gil. Either you trust me, or you don't. Which is it going to be?'

Gil knew from his face that this was her last chance. If she didn't level with him now, she would lose the only ally she had. She couldn't afford that. And she didn't want it.

She let out a long breath and said, 'I'm sorry. You're dead right; we've got to trust each other, or we won't get anywhere.' She managed a small smile. 'Start again?' she offered.

Jonas hesitated, then nodded. 'Start again. So: who's Robert?'

Gil told him about the tomb, the worn carvings and the inscription. She also owned up to the feeling she had experienced, that had sent her running out of the church and back to the road. When she finished, Jonas's eyes narrowed.

'There was a name . . . I came across it years ago; I think we were doing some kind of local history project at school. L – something. Lis – Los—' He snapped his fingers in frustration as he tried to remember. Suddenly his eyes lit up. 'Leece! That was it.' He flopped down on the window seat, where Gil had dropped *The Historic Families of Norfolk*, peered at the index, then flicked pages very fast. 'There!' One finger jabbed. 'There's a load of them, starting with Sir Hubert, who went on the crusades. Let's see . . . his son was Guy, then after him there was Stephen, then Henry, and then—' He looked at Gil triumphantly. 'Bull's-eye. Sir Robert Leece.'

Gil bent to look over his shoulder. Sir Robert, it appeared, had been a baron and a very influential landowner. And his wife –

Surprised and disappointed, she said, 'It can't be him. This Robert's wife was called Elaine.'

Jonas had been reading on, and he shook his head. 'Elaine died young. He married again. His second wife was called Joanna.'

Joanna . . . Iohan . . . Was one a mediaeval spelling of the other? It was possible, Gil thought.

'When did they die?' she asked.

'It doesn't say. In fact . . .' Jonas finished reading the entry, just to be sure, 'the whole family just seems to stop.

After Robert and Joanna, there's no mention of any more Leeces at all. That's weird!'

'Not necessarily,' Gil pointed out. 'Maybe Robert didn't have any children.'

'Yeah, maybe. But it doesn't *say* that the family died out. You'd expect some mention of it, wouldn't you? Even if they were all wiped out by the plague, or something, some record would have been made.'

'Can you remember anything about your school project?' Gil asked.

'Not really. Just that the Leeces lived at the manor house that was demolished ages ago.'

'What about your teacher?'

He laughed. 'Fine, if you can track her down in New Zealand! This was at the village school; it shut down a year after I left, and she emigrated. No; there's only one person I can think of who might know about this. And he's the one person who won't give us an answer.'

'Uncle Alan?'

'Right. Back to square one, in other words.' Jonas glowered out at the windy garden. 'I wondered about Mum; whether she knows, and whether she'd tell us if she did. But she might say something to Granfa. I don't think it's worth the risk.'

Gil agreed. She didn't know whether she ought to voice what was in her mind. But she had promised to level with him.

'I think we ought to take another look round the old church,' she said.

She didn't know how Jonas would react. She half expected him to say no, or at least dither, but instead he swung round and said, 'Then let's not hang around – Mum won't be back for a bit, so no one's going to ask any awkward questions. Come on!'

Seeing the phone in the hall, Gil remembered that her parents were going to call this morning. She so desperately wanted news of Biddy, and if there was no one here . . . But surely, she told herself, this was more important. She was trying to *do* something. It had to be better than just waiting helplessly around.

'I'll get my mobile.' She ran up to her room and grabbed the phone. Then – though if anyone had asked her, she couldn't have said why she did it – she snatched up the little carving that Jonas called Touchwood. *Touch him for triple good luck – head, heart and feet* . . . Gil thrust Touchwood into her coat pocket, and hurried downstairs again.

8

The wind was roaring in the pines as Gil and Jonas approached the ancient church. Tattered clouds scudded overhead, so low that they almost seemed to be brushing the tree tops, and against their grey background the ruin had an ominous look.

At the lych gate Jonas stopped, as if he was afraid to go through. Gil, too, remembered her previous visit, and wondered if what they were doing was pointless. She was tempted to suggest that they turn round and go home; but abruptly Jonas snapped back to earth and walked into the churchyard. She hesitated a bare moment, then followed.

It took them a few minutes to find the tomb. Gil was sure she remembered exactly where it was, but she did not remember the tricky scramble among rotten beams and fallen chunks of masonry to get to it.

'Some more of the building might have collapsed since you were last here,' Jonas said, looking uneasily up at the tops of the broken walls. 'We'd better be careful. Don't even speak too loudly.'

Gil shivered, remembering Alan's earlier warning. They crouched down beside the tomb and Jonas peered at the worn lettering.

'I'll bet anything this *is* a version of Joanna,' he murmured after a few moments. 'But the rest . . . it's impossible to read.' He straightened and stared around. 'OK. Let's start exploring, and see if we can find anything else to do with the Leeces.'

Starting from the tomb, they began to work their way slowly and systematically around the crumbling walls. After an hour, though, they had found nothing, and at last Gil stopped and sat down on a pile of rubble.

'This is useless,' she said. 'If Robert and Joanna really were the last of the family, then any other tombs have got to be older than theirs, so they'll be in an even worse state. We probably couldn't even recognise one if we found it.'

'Not necessarily,' Jonas argued. 'There might be something in a less damaged part of the church, in which case it'll be in better condition, not worse.'

'Well, the least damaged part is through there.' Gil nodded at an archway choked with ferocious-looking brambles. 'If you want to try getting through that lot, you're welcome!'

He wasn't daunted. 'I can probably get through from the outside. Worth a go, anyway. You coming?'

She shook her head. 'I want to sit down for a bit; I'm whacked.'

'OK. If I get through, I'll call out.'

'Not loudly!'

'All right; I'll whisper, then.' He grinned, and went. Gil shifted to a less uncomfortable position and waited, her gaze roaming around the gloomy interior. The noise of the wind was muffled to a dull grumble by the stone walls, but an occasional gust hooted eerily through the empty window holes. The light was getting worse, too; when she looked up, she saw that the grey of the clouds was darker and more solid. If they didn't watch it they could get caught out in a downpour . . . Gil got up and moved towards the bramble barrier.

'Jonas?' She put her face as close to the tangle as she could without getting scratched. 'Are you there yet? It's going to belt down with rain by the look of it.'

There was no answer, and no sound of anyone moving on the other side of the thicket.

'Jonas!' Then, remembering, she hastily dropped her voice. 'If we hang around much longer, we'll get soaked. Come on. We can always come back another time. Jonas . . .?' She paused, listening, but still there was no response. If there was another way into that part of the church he must have found it by now. Maybe there wasn't, and he was on his way back?

Gil had just turned to look towards the church's main doorway when from behind her came a soft, muted *swish*.

'Jonas?' She spun again, expecting to see his face peering through the bramble thicket. There was no one there. But a second later the swishing sound was followed by another, still behind her, though she was looking in a different direction.

Gil's skin started to prickle. 'Who's there? Jonas, is it you?'

No answer; no sign of movement. Her heart started to thump. 'Whoever you are, I heard you,' she said, trying to sound confident. 'There's no point hiding.'

Still nothing. The swishing sound had stopped, but she was sure she hadn't imagined it. It occurred to her that it had sounded very much like something sweeping across the stone floor. A broom, maybe. Or the hem of a long skirt . . .

Gil was suddenly very anxious either to find Jonas or to get out of the church as fast as possible. She made an impulsive move towards the brambles, as if by sheer willpower she could push her way through them. She couldn't. One leg brushed against a coiling stem, and a row of thorns instantly hooked into her jeans. She pulled back but the thorns clung, tearing small holes; then another stem caught her jacket sleeve and the tiny barbs scratched her hand.

'*Oww!*' Gil sucked her hand as the pain effectively squashed the panicky feeling and brought her back to earth with a thump. Angrily she jerked herself free, and was about to forget this attempt and head for the main door when something pale moved deep in the brambles. She froze, staring. The shape had vanished. But she could have sworn that it was a human hand . . .

Then a voice hissed, '*Quickly!*'

'What?' Gil jumped violently, turned again — and saw the red-haired girl. She was several metres away, peering like a small, feral animal from behind one of the stone pillars that had once held up a part of the church roof. As Gil's eyes widened, she hissed, '*Quickly!*' a second time, emphasising it with a sharp, beckoning gesture. Then she dodged behind the pillar and was gone.

'Hey! Come back!' Gil made to go after the child, but a clumsy move brought her arm into contact with the brambles again. Thorns snagged; she felt them sting—

And another, far more intense pain shot through her arm as four or five barbs bit deep into her wrist.

Gil yelped and tore free, stumbling several paces and nearly falling over as her foot turned on the broken floor. From somewhere, though she couldn't have said where, came what sounded like a heavy sigh.

Shock, pain and fright had set Gil's pulse racing, and the sound was the last straw. Holding her wrist (it stung; it really *stung*), she made a scrambling rush for the gaping door arch. As she burst outside, Jonas appeared round the side of the building.

'No good,' he said when he saw her. 'If anything, the brambles are even . . .' The words petered out as he saw her face and the fact that she was clutching her arm. 'What's happened?'

Gil gulped down a huge breath. 'I just saw the red-haired girl!'

'You *did*? Where?'

'Inside – she called out to me, but then she disappeared again!'

Jonas started to make a move back towards the church and with a renewed surge of fright Gil realised that she didn't want him to. 'No!' she said sharply, then forced herself to calm down and be rational. 'There's no point,' she added. 'She's gone. I don't think we'll find her again.'

He swore under his breath. 'This is getting weirder . . . But you said she called out. What did she say?'

' "Quickly". Just that; nothing else. I don't know what she meant. I was going to go after her, but then . . .' Gil held out her arm, and saw with a small shock that blood was welling up between her grasping fingers and dripping on the grass.

'What have you done?' Jonas's voice sharpened anxiously.

'It was the brambles; they ripped my arm. But I don't think it's much.'

'Better let me have a look.' Jonas took her arm, surprisingly gently, and gingerly she lifted her hand away.

'Whoo!' He winced in sympathy. 'Just surface damage, I think, but it's nasty enough. You'd better clean it thoroughly when we get home.'

'It really *hurts*,' she said. 'And the thorns weren't that big.'

'It doesn't take much with brambles; they're vicious. I fell into a bush once, when I was little, and of course I panicked and tried to thrash my way out.' He grinned ruefully. 'I can still remember the pain!'

'Yes, well, I'd rather forget it, thanks!'

A drop of rain fell fatly on the ground nearby, then another. 'Uh-oh,' said Jonas. 'We'd better shift.'

'What about that girl?'

'You said yourself, you don't think we'll find her again. But maybe we can find something else in Granfa's books. Because I'm *certain* he knows who she is.'

Gil nodded. More drops of rain fell; she could feel it on her hair now.

'Here it comes,' said Jonas. 'We'd better run!'

Rose was still out shopping when they reached April House, so there was no one to ask where they had been or fuss over the fact that they were both soaked to the skin by the downpour. Gil grabbed a shower, as much to warm herself up as anything else. Her wrist was still bleeding when she went into the shower, and she began to wonder if the wound was serious. But by the time she emerged the bleeding had stopped, so she simply took a sticking plaster from the cabinet to cover it.

She hadn't noticed earlier, but the marks of the thorns' assault were an odd shape. Instead of straight scratches – she had a few of those, too, so she could compare – they were crescent-shaped, and there were four of them in an almost straight line, spaced very evenly. They were larger than the other scratches, too. In fact they did not look like bramble scratches at all. They looked more like the marks of fingernails. Probably she had dug her own nails into her wrist in the first shock, she thought ruefully; in which case she'd done more damage than the brambles had. Her wrist still throbbed a bit, but she stuck the plaster on carefully, put a piece of surgical tape over it for good measure (being a retired doctor, Alan had a well stocked medicine cabinet) and went downstairs to find Jonas.

He was in the study again, and he had taken several books down from the shelves and piled them on a table. The room felt very cold; rain streamed down the window, almost blotting out the view of the garden, and Gil wished they could have switched on the electric fire that stood in the hearth where a coal fire used to burn.

'We can hide these books upstairs and look at them when no one else is around,' he said, glancing up from his search of the shelves. 'But we'll have to be careful not to take too many, or Granfa might notice.'

Gil nodded. Her wrist was itching as well as throbbing now, and she resisted the urge to scratch it hard. As Jonas picked another book out, she looked idly around the room and her gaze came to rest on several framed photographs on the mantelpiece. Family pictures, by the look of them. In one she recognised a younger Rose, clear-eyed and pretty before her accident, with a little red-haired boy who must be Jonas. There had been a third person in the picture – an elbow was just visible – but someone had carefully cut the photo to remove them.

Jonas saw her looking, guessed what she was wondering and said, 'My dad. After he left Mum, Granfa wouldn't have a picture of him in the house.'

He sounded casual, but Gil detected the anger – or pain? – underlying his words. 'What does your dad look like?' she asked.

He shrugged. 'I can't remember, really. Mum says I take after him, but I don't know. Don't see how I could, really, with this red hair.'

'Don't you ever hear from him?'

'No,' said Jonas shortly. 'He pays maintenance through a solicitor, but that's all. I think he's remarried. Can we change the subject?'

'Right.' Gil hid the sympathy in her eyes. 'Sorry.' She stared at the photos again. In the middle of the display was an older picture, black and white, showing two grinning boys in old-fashioned shorts, long socks and knitted jerkins. 'Who are they?' she asked, wanting to get on safer ground.

'Uh?' Jonas looked, then smiled faintly. 'Believe it or not, the one on the left's Granfa, when he was a kid. The other one's his brother, but I can't remember his name.'

'Your . . . great-uncle?' She looked more closely. 'They're very alike. Faces, anyway; their hair's totally different.'

'Yeah. The brother was a couple of years younger, I think. But he died young. Quite a lot of kids did in those days, so Granfa says. Illnesses and things . . . it's probably why Granfa wanted to be a doctor. Look, the photos are very interesting and all that, but we've got more important things to think about. Mum'll be back soon, and I want to get these books hidden.'

'Sorry,' Gil said again. She glanced at the photo one last time, and something struck her about the two boys' hair. Alan's looked jet black. But his brother's . . . You couldn't be sure in a black-and-white picture, of course, but it looked as if his hair could have been as red as her own and Jonas's and Biddy's. A Granger family trait. Just like the mysterious little girl . . .

She was jolted away from her thoughts as Jonas dumped three heavy books into her arms. 'Hide these in your room, and I'll put the rest in mine.' There was the sound of a car engine outside. 'That's Mum – quick, before she comes in.'

Gil forgot about Alan's dead brother, and hurried towards the stairs.

Gil's parents phoned at lunchtime. There was no news, good or bad; Biddy was still unconscious, her father said, and was to have more tests tomorrow. He added that Mum was bearing up but was under tremendous strain. He was strained, too, though he tried to put on a brave voice for Gil, and when she said goodbye and hung up,

Gil felt desperately depressed; so much so that she didn't have the heart to start going through the books that were hidden in her room. Jonas tried to persuade her and she snapped at him, then she went upstairs, locked her door and lay on the bed, staring at nothing in particular. She wasn't just depressed, she felt incredibly tired, too. Not surprising really, after last night. But though she longed to sleep for a while, she found she couldn't. She simply lay, staring, without the energy even to think.

She only got up when Rose came to see if she was all right and to say that dinner would be ready soon. Alan was due back at any time, and Gil didn't want to arouse his suspicions. So she went reluctantly downstairs.

Jonas obviously had something to tell her, but Gil felt too weary and listless to want to hear it, so she hung around the kitchen, where Rose's presence blocked him from saying anything. Dinner was to be roast chicken with sage and onion stuffing from a packet, which even Rose found hard to mess up; Gil volunteered to look after the vegetables, and so Alan arrived home to a delicious smell from the Aga. Over the meal he told a couple of amusing stories about the conference, and Rose chatted about her shopping trip, but Jonas was restlessly silent and Gil now felt so tired that she thought she could easily have flopped forward with her face on her plate and slept for ten hours. Her wrist still itched, too. But if Alan noticed he said nothing, and Rose seemed to think that Gil was simply worn out with worrying about Biddy. All Gil wanted was to finish eating and go to bed.

However, there was an unpleasant surprise in store for her. When dinner was over she tried to do the washing up, but she was so sleepy that halfway through it Rose told her firmly to stop being helpful and go to bed. Gil went, gratefully. But as she climbed the stairs she began to feel queasy, and by the time she was halfway along the landing to her gable, her stomach was churning horribly. She only just made it to the bathroom in time, and was violently sick down the loo. The spasms went on and on until there was nothing left to throw up, and by the time they finally stopped Gil's skin was covered with ice-cold sweat and she felt as weak as a kitten. It was all she could do to totter to her room and collapse, fully dressed, into bed.

What on earth had caused *that*? Unless the chicken was off . . . but it had smelled fine, and it certainly wasn't undercooked; Rose was much more inclined to burn things. Was anyone else ill? Or was it just her? And her wrist wasn't just itching now: it was *hurting*.

Gil tried to sit up and discovered that she didn't have the strength. She was sweating again, and shivering too. What was the *matter* with her?

She had no answer to the question, and felt too ill to look for one. Turning over, she buried her face in the pillow, and sank into a heavy sleep.

★   ★   ★

Gil had a nightmare. In it, she was stumbling in darkness over a sandy beach littered with huge chunks of fallen masonry. Someone was with her, but she didn't know who it was because the dark was so intense that she could see nothing. Sometimes she thought it was Jonas, sometimes not; but it didn't matter. Much more important was the fact that someone else was following them. That someone wasn't far behind; she – somehow, Gil knew it was a she – wasn't catching up, but at the same time Gil couldn't run fast enough to get away. She *wanted* to get away; wanted it more than anything, because she was very, very frightened of whoever was following.

Suddenly, in the weird way of dreams, there was an old lych gate in the middle of the beach, and before she could stop herself Gil ran through it. The sand vanished; she could still hear the sea but it was more distant now, and its roar sounded like many human voices. *A choir*, she thought. *They're singing to warn me*. That thought was crazy and she pushed it away. Her companion, who might or might not have been Jonas, wasn't there any more. But her unknown follower was. And now that they had passed through the lych gate, she was catching up . . .

Then, with no warning at all, Gil ran straight into a solid wall. Surprisingly, it didn't hurt. In fact the wall was soft, like a huge piece of foam, and when she opened her mouth in astonishment she tasted sugar—

And woke up.

The shock of snapping out of the dream so suddenly was bad enough – but it was nothing compared to the shock that followed when she realised where she was. Not in bed. Not even in April House. She was standing, barefoot, in a narrow lane, with the wind whistling in scrubby pine trees and moonlight flickering fitfully beyond scudding clouds.

A strange, wailing sound joined with the whistle of the wind, and Gil realised that it had come from her own mouth. It was a cry of fear, of bewilderment; panic rose in her chest, hurting her ribs, as her reeling mind tried to find something, *anything*, that would tell her this was not real.

Pinch yourself! The thought came instantly, and Gil pinched the soft flesh of her upper arms as hard as she could. It hurt, but nothing changed, and in a surge of wild terror she started to slap and pummel herself, frantically willing the scene around her to melt into the familiar contours of the gable bedroom as she really, *really* woke up.

Only when she found herself on all fours on the road, knees and palms grazed and her nose only centimetres from the tarmac, did she face the fact that this wasn't a dream. Painfully she clambered to her feet and stood shivering and unsteady in the middle of the lane, trying to make herself calm down and think clearly. Thicker clouds had covered the moon now, but the sky to her right reflected a pale band of light, enough to make out shapes and contours, and she thought she knew pretty well where she was. The reflected glow was from the sea, and ahead the lane curved to the left. She remembered that curve, and the two trees on the bend that had crooked trunks. She was about half a mile from April House . . . and less distance than that from the ruined church.

Gil's fear, which had begun to recede as she got her wits under control, came back in an acute surge as she realised that she must have been deliberately heading for St. Osyth's. But why – and, more frighteningly, *how*? Had she been sleepwalking? Or had she been awake and aware, but suffered some sort of mental blackout that had made her forget the chunk of time between going to bed and finding herself here in the lane? Both possibilities had awful implications, because they suggested that something other than her own will had been driving her. Or calling her . . .

Calling . . . Gil flicked a quick, jumpy glance along the lane where it faded into the gloom ahead. Nothing moved there – that shape was only a bush by the roadside, she *knew* it was – but her imagination started to race at a dangerous level as she stared into the dark. *Don't panic*, she told herself ferociously. *You're here, this is happening, and panicking won't change anything. Just turn round and start walking back the way you came. Slowly. Calmly. Come on; do it!*

The tarmac was cold and rough on her bare feet, and

she tried to concentrate on that as she turned around to face the direction of April House. She started to walk, and though she was screaming inwardly to look back over her shoulder, she wouldn't let herself weaken. *Come on, Gil. It isn't far. Come on!*

Then from behind her a voice said, 'Gillian.' And a small, icily cold hand slipped between her fingers and gripped them.

9

Gil's shriek rang shrilly into the night and shock jolted through her like an electric current. She spun round—

The red-haired girl was there, staring up at her with huge eyes. Gil's violent start had broken the contact between them and the child's hands hung loosely at her sides. She said, 'Please don't be frightened of me.'

Gil's brain whirled and latched on to the first thought that jumped at her out of the muddle. The girl had said *Gillian* – 'Who told you my name?' she demanded.

The girl didn't answer the question. 'You came back,' she stated flatly.

'I didn't! Something happened to me; I didn't mean to come, I must have – oh, never *mind*!' Gil could feel her nerves winding up towards breaking point. 'Who are you? Why do you keep following me around? What do you *want*?'

'They've taken your sister to London,' said the girl. 'But no one there can help her. I know.'

'*How* do you know?' Gil all but screamed at her. '*How?*'

'Because I do. You can help her, Gillian. I can tell you—'

Another voice snapped, 'No!'

The boy came out of the night as suddenly as if he had appeared from another dimension. He was a little older than the girl, but his hair was the same fiery red, and Gil saw instantly the similarity in their faces. There was no similarity in the boy's manner, though. He was angry, and he grasped the girl by the upper arms, shaking her.

'I said *no*, Elaine! You mustn't tell!' The girl began to protest and he shook her again, viciously. 'Hear me, and be *quiet*! Or you know what will happen to you!'

'Leave her alone!' Gil said angrily as the girl started to cry. 'Who do you think you are, bullying her like that?'

The boy let go of the girl's arms and turned on Gil. 'I'm her brother,' he retorted. 'And she must do as I say!'

'Oh, must she?' Buried in Gil's mind was the thought that this whole encounter was horribly surreal. But she couldn't grasp the thought, couldn't bring herself back to earth. 'Now look,' she went on, her own anger rising, 'if she says she can help my sister, then you're not going to stop her! Do you understand?'

The boy laughed in her face. '*You're* the one who doesn't understand,' he said contemptuously.

'Then you'd better explain, hadn't you?' *Explain why I'm standing out here in the middle of the night, talking to two weird kids who might not even exist. I don't think this is really happening. I think I'm going mad . . .*

Then abruptly the boy smiled. 'All right,' he said. 'I will explain. But you must come with us. You must see for yourself.' He glanced at his sister. 'Isn't that so, Elaine?'

The girl put a clenched fist to her mouth. 'Edmund . . . I don't . . .'

'It *is* so! *She* must see Gillian! Repeat to me what Father said before he boarded the ship!'

Elaine's small face crumpled, as if she were about to cry again. In little more than a whisper she replied, 'He said . . . we must be good, and do what she tells us. Or – or we'll be taken away and we won't ever see him again . . .'

'That's right. So.' Edmund looked at Gil once more, and held out a hand. 'Come with us. Now.'

Their gazes met and clashed. Even in the gloom Gil saw that Edmund's eyes were a very bright blue, almost unnaturally bright. They held her; she wanted to look away but found she could not.

'Wait a minute . . .' Her mind was floundering. 'Who is this . . . this *she*?'

Edmund smiled again. 'The only one who can help your sister.' His hand flicked, impatiently. 'We'll take you to her – but only if you come with us *now*.'

He made a quick, unexpected movement, and his fingers clamped round Gil's wrist. It was the one that the brambles had torn, and she winced as pain shot through her arm. 'Please—' she said. Her head was reeling; she felt dizzy—

'Now!' Edmund repeated again. 'Or she won't help you. And then what will become of your sister?'

Gil swayed as the world around her seemed to lurch and twist in on itself. Edmund's stare was burning into her brain; his eyes seemed to be getting brighter . . . She tried to find words to argue, but they wouldn't come, and though instinct was screaming at her to turn and run as she had never run in her life, she couldn't make her legs do what she wanted. Elaine had backed away until she was no more than a shadow in the dark. Edmund tugged at Gil's wrist, gently, but with an insistence that she didn't have the will to resist.

'Now,' he said for the fourth time.

Gil said, 'Yes . . .'

She could almost feel the old church's brooding presence reaching out of the night, and she struggled to make herself stop walking and shout, *This is enough, I won't go any further!* But though the words were in her head, they didn't seem to reach her mouth and throat. And her feet kept moving, one after the other, again and again, every step taking her closer to the ruin.

Edmund still held her wrist, but his grip was lighter now, as if he knew that she wasn't going to run away. Elaine padded silently ahead of them. She had not spoken since they set off, and she didn't look back. By now, Gil felt almost completely disconnected from reality. Every so often a glimmer of rational thought broke through, such as the knowledge that if only a car would come along the lane, it would break the trance and she could escape. But no car came, and the hope faded, and she stumbled helplessly on.

When she saw the lych gate she remembered the nightmare she had had before she woke up to find herself here. She desperately did *not* want to walk through the broken-down portal. But Edmund was leading her and she couldn't protest. Swimming in her mind was the image of Biddy lying unconscious in the sand dunes, with that terrible, deadly flush reddening her cheeks . . .

The hard road under her feet changed to damp grass and, blinking, she looked up at the ruin of St. Osyth's, grim against the night sky. *I don't want to go in there . . .* She struggled again to argue, but all that came out was a peculiar mewing sound, and Edmund took no notice.

Near the main door arch Elaine stopped and waited for them to catch up. 'Edmund . . .' she began.

Her brother interrupted her. 'Go on ahead and tell her that we've come,' he ordered.

'But—'

'*Remember what Father told us!*'

For a moment Elaine stared at him with mute appeal. Then she shook her head in defeat, turned and ran into the church. Edmund and Gil followed more slowly, and he led her through the rubble, finding his way easily and surely. At first Gil thought he was leading her towards the brambles where she had torn herself yesterday. Then she realised: they were going to the ancient tomb she had found; the tomb of Robert and Joanna Leece.

Elaine was standing by the tomb, looking very small and vulnerable. Gil thought she had started to cry again. Edmund led her to the stone monument, and when they reached it he stretched out his free hand and laid it on the carved, eroded figures on the top of the slab.

Gil expected something diabolical; expected the slab to slide aside with an ominous rumble, and *something* to emerge from the tomb below. But nothing happened. Then she saw Edmund's expression: a terrible combination of grief and bitterness and – she struggled to interpret through the fog in her mind – and *longing*, as if he had lost everything he had ever loved in the world. His hand was resting on the figure of Sir Robert, fingers splayed over his praying stone hands. And Elaine *was* crying . . .

A sweet voice said, 'Poor, poor child . . .'

Dreamily, Gil turned round. At the same moment the moon appeared beyond a gap in the clouds, and a cold silver glow lit up the church. A tall woman was standing in the shimmer of the moonlight. She was grey and vague and insubstantial; she had a face, but Gil could make out no detail. Her head was an unnatural shape, rising almost to a point. Something about that shape was familiar. For a moment Gil couldn't recall. Then—

A long shadow, lying like an accusing finger across the moonlit garden; growing as it moved towards her window. And a tapering head, with shoulders beneath . . .

The muscles of Gil's arms and legs locked rigid as the memory slammed into her mind and almost broke her trance. She tried to back away but couldn't move. Then Edmund took a tighter hold on her wrist and pain flared through her arm.

'Nn . . .' She was trying to say *No*, but all that came out was an ugly gargling sound. The figure stepped – no; it *glided* – towards her, and from the folds of what looked like a long robe or gown, two pale, slim hands reached out, palms up, in a gesture of welcome.

'Poor child,' the sweet voice said again. Gil stared, transfixed. Her only conscious thought was that, if she could only make out the grey woman's face clearly, it would be incredibly beautiful. Then the pale hands reached further, reached her fingers, and linked with them.

'You are very afraid.' *Oh, that voice was so gentle . . .* 'But there is nothing to fear, Gillian. Trust in me. Let me comfort you. Come to me, now. Come . . .'

A fragment of Gil's mind was still free of the spell, and it shrieked silently, *Run! Just RUN!* But the trance was too powerful. And now she could make out the grey woman's eyes. Huge eyes, huge and dark like deep pools, with a strange, shining light in their depths that went on and on for ever.

She sighed. She took a step forward, then a second. Now she was so close to the grey woman that she should have been able to feel the folds of her long gown. But she felt nothing.

'There, there, my child,' the woman crooned softly. 'Look at me. I will help you. Trust in me.'

She stooped forward, leaning over Gil until her shape shut out the sky.

'You're wearing a headdress,' Gil said dreamily. 'That's why you looked so strange when I saw you in the garden . . .'

She thought the woman smiled. 'What lovely hair you have,' she said. 'Such a fine colour. So red.'

She touched Gil's hair, stroking it. Gil thought she could hear Elaine crying again. 'Your hair is like a beautiful flame. You are full of *life*.'

Her face came closer. For one instant Gil saw it clearly. The woman *was* smiling. Her smile was—

Evil . . .

Like a light being switched off, Gil's consciousness blanked out.

She was lying face down, and something was digging painfully into her ribs. She started to turn over and something else dug into her stomach. Her body felt stiff with cold, and the muscles of her arms and legs ached as though she had been on a marathon run. What on earth . . .

Gil's eyes opened and she found herself staring at a grey surface, two centimetres from the end of her nose. As she groggily raised her head, her eyes focused and she saw that it was a slab of stone. Her brain struggled to work that out but couldn't, so she tried to sit up, and immediately felt herself begin to slide. Her hands grabbed for a hold, her legs and body slithered; instinctively she twisted round to save herself, then suddenly she slid right off an edge—

And landed with an ungraceful thump on the floor of the ruined church, with her back against the tomb of Robert and Joanna Leece.

Shock jogged Gil fully awake, and right on its heels came a breath-snatching wave of sheer disbelief. What was she *doing* here? She couldn't remember coming, didn't know why she had come, or how, or with who – there was no memory at all in her head to give her the smallest clue. Yet here she was, without shoes or a jacket, with a chilly dawn just breaking . . . What time must it be? She tried vainly to work it out, then recalled that she had a watch and looked at it. Just gone six. Her heart punched against her ribs and she thought, *Oh, God, what's happening to me?*

Suddenly she had an idea, and she grasped desperately at it. Maybe this was something to do with Jonas; maybe they had come here together for some reason, and they'd got too tired and fallen asleep, and he was around here somewhere? She called his name in a quavering voice. But there was no answer, no sign of anyone or anything moving, and however hard she tried she couldn't convince herself that was the answer. Jonas wasn't here. She was on her own. But *how* had it happened?

She had a vague feeling that she ought to feel afraid. But she didn't; all she knew was a strange, dull sensation of unreality, as if she was in a dream world that didn't truly exist. Only the fact that she was stiff with cramp and cold, and her body ached where the unforgiving stone had been pressing into her, forced her to believe that it wasn't a dream.

Home. She wanted to go home. But proper home was more than a hundred miles away; all she could do was go back to April House. Then as soon as she thought of April House, she had a sudden and powerful conviction that no one else must find out about this. She had to keep it a secret; even Jonas mustn't know. She had to get back, before they woke up and realised she was missing . . .

Like a swimmer launching into deep water, Gil pushed herself away from the tomb and stumbled groggily across the church's broken floor towards the door arch. It was incredibly hard going; her legs seemed to have no strength in them, and she ached from head to foot, the way you did if you were just recovering from a bad bout of flu. All her body wanted was to curl up and go back to sleep. But she must not sleep. She must go back. She must keep her secret . . .

She reached the doorway, paused for a few seconds to get her breath back, then set off with grim determination towards the lane.

Gil reached the house before anyone was up and about to see her. The back door was unlocked – which meant she must have let herself out – and by the time she was halfway up the stairs the last of her strength was draining away, so that she could hardly pull herself to the top. Again she longed just to curl up and sleep. But she could hear the faint sound of a radio from the direction of Rose's room. Rose would be getting up any minute. She *must* get to the east gable.

She made it, fell into bed and knew nothing until she felt someone shaking her shoulder.

'Gil?' It was Jonas's voice. 'Come on, wake up! It's gone eleven.'

'Uh?' Gil struggled into consciousness and blinked blearily. 'Gone wha . . . ?'

'Eleven. Mum said to let you sleep in, but there are limits. And we need to talk.'

She looked at him, her eyes not yet focusing properly, and felt a surge of resentment. Who did he think he was, waking her up when she wanted to sleep? *He* might want to talk, but she didn't. Whatever he had to say, she wasn't interested.

She said coldly, 'Go away.'

'Gil! Come on; what's the matter with you?' Jonas

paused. 'Did you sleep badly last night, or something?'

'Mind your own business,' Gil retorted. 'Just leave me alone.'

She turned over, burying her face in the pillow. For a few moments there was silence, and she was starting to hope that Jonas *had* gone away when he said, 'All right, if that's the mood you're in.' She heard his footsteps heading towards the door. Then:

'By the way, your dad rang earlier. If you're interested.'

'Why should I be interested?'

'*Why?*' Jonas sounded shocked. 'Well for one thing, you *might* want to know how your sister is!'

Biddy. Her sister. Biddy was ill, in hospital in London. It didn't mean a thing to Gil, but she didn't bother to say so. She just shrugged, still hiding her face. She could feel Jonas's reaction; a mixture of bewilderment and disgust that was like a knife cutting the air, but she didn't care about that, either. Then his feet thudded on the carpet, and the door banged as he went out.

Gil turned her head enough to breathe properly and for a long time lay where she was, her eyes wide open but staring at nothing. Somewhere inside her was the thought that what she had said to Jonas was very wrong, but she couldn't quite grasp and make sense of it. She *did* care about Biddy . . . didn't she? Surely, as recently as yesterday, she . . .

The thought faded into a vast yawn. She was so *tired*. Must have spent half the night dreaming, though she couldn't remember any of her dreams now. In fact she couldn't remember anything since she came upstairs last night. Just *tired*. That was all that was wrong with her.

Her eyelids drooped and she went back to sleep.

It was after one by the time Gil woke properly. When she looked at her watch she could hardly believe it, and she scrambled out of bed (what was she doing still dressed? She *really* must have been whacked last night!) and hurried downstairs.

There was no sign of Alan or Rose, but Jonas was in the kitchen making himself a sandwich. He looked at her with angry suspicion.

'Oh, you've finally decided to surface, have you?'

'Sorry.' Gil yawned. She couldn't seem to stop yawning. And she ached, too; all over, as if she had been doing a lot of strenuous exercise. 'I don't know what's the matter with me . . . Is everyone else out?'

'Mum's shopping again for all the things she forgot yesterday, and Granfa's taken his car in for a service.' Jonas's expression was downright peculiar, she thought. Anyone would think she was a complete stranger to him.

'Oh, right,' she said; then, hopefully, 'I suppose Mum and Dad haven't phoned with any news?'

Jonas opened his mouth to explode at her – then before the words could come out, he hastily bit them back. Keeping his voice carefully neutral, he replied, 'Your dad rang at about ten-thirty.'

126

'What?' Gil's eyes widened. 'What did he say? Why didn't someone wake me up?'

'We . . . thought it was better to let you sleep. Granfa talked to your dad. There still isn't any news.'

'Oh, God . . .' Gil turned away, biting her lip. She was not aware that Jonas was watching her intently. 'Where is Dad? Can I call him back?'

'He was on his mobile, but he said he and your mum were going to the hospital so he'd have to switch it off. He'll ring back when they come out.'

Gil nodded. She wanted to cry but there wasn't any real reason for it; no news, at least, wasn't bad news. *So* tired . . . She scratched her wrist without realising she was doing it, then scratched at her neck, which was itching too.

'How are the bramble wounds?' Jonas asked.

Something clicked in Gil's brain and suddenly she didn't want to tell him about it. 'They're OK,' she said. 'Fine.'

'You've still got a plaster on.'

'Yeah. I might as well leave it till it comes off by itself.' She scratched again and was answered by a violent throbbing up the length of her arm.

'Don't you think you ought to take a look at it now, just to make sure it's not gone septic or anything?'

Annoyance flared irrationally in Gil and she snapped back at him. 'Oh, stop fussing, will you! You're as bad as Aunt Rose!' The angry flare grew, swelled; and abruptly it overflowed. 'Look,' Gil added savagely, 'I'm perfectly all right, and I *hate* being fussed at, and I *don't* want to talk about anything! So just *get off my back*!'

She stormed out of the kitchen before Jonas had time to respond, and stamped across the hall and back upstairs to the east gable. Jonas was a *pain*, poking his nose into everything, probing and questioning. What she felt or thought was nothing to do with him; nothing at all! She just wanted to be left in *peace*.

She slammed her bedroom door even harder than Jonas had done earlier, and threw herself face down on the bed.

10

Gil's parents rang back late in the afternoon. Gil had been sleeping again, but she heard Rose calling, 'Gil! Phone!' from the landing below, and she nearly fell headlong down the stairs in her rush to take the call.

Biddy was no better, but no worse, and the tests were still 'inconclusive'. Both her parents sounded utterly drained and exhausted, but though Gil's heart went out to them all, a small and muffled little voice deep inside her mind was saying: *So what? Why should I care? It doesn't matter to me.* And every few moments throughout the call, she had a mad and terrible urge to start laughing. By the time she hung up, she was in a state of total confusion – but as she put the phone receiver down, the dimensions of the hall seemed suddenly to lurch and distort around her. Gil swayed, almost losing her balance . . . then the sensation vanished and she found herself leaning forward with her palms splayed on the hall table, and the confusion was gone. She remembered only that she had talked to Mum and Dad and that there was no news worth a mention. Fine. No problem. It didn't matter, anyway. She'd just go back to her room.'

If Gil had been in her normal state of mind, she would have noticed the strangeness of Jonas's behaviour towards her for the rest of that day and evening. Whenever she was around, he acted as if he was walking on eggshells and trying not to break them. He hardly said a word to her, and when he did it was about something bland and trivial, so that she couldn't possibly take offence. But though he didn't speak much, he watched her in the sort of way that someone might watch a ferocious dog; mistrustful, and waiting for the sudden attack. Gil wasn't even aware of it. Alan, though, was. He said nothing to either Jonas or Gil. But he thought his own thoughts . . .

As dusk fell, Gil began to feel impatient, and eager to get the evening over and done with as soon as possible. She didn't want any dinner – she wasn't the least bit hungry – and a kind of feverish excitement was bubbling under the surface of her mind. She wanted everyone else to go to bed. She wanted all the house lights to be turned off, so that she had the night to herself. And then . . .

But she didn't know what 'and then' actually was. She only knew that there was something she had to do. Something important, that must be kept secret from everyone else. To avoid suspicion she tried not to let her impatience show, but when they all went to the sitting room to watch television her feet were constantly fidgeting, as if they wanted to carry her away at a run. Time seemed to drag endlessly; she kept looking at her watch, then at the mantelpiece clock to make sure that the watch had not stopped. If anyone had asked, she couldn't have told them what was on the TV, but at last

Rose stood up, switched the set off and stretched her arms.

'I'm for bed,' she said, and smiled at Gil. 'You ought to go up, too, love. You look worn out.'

'Yes,' said Gil. 'I am pretty tired.'

'Go on, then. Would you like me to bring you up a hot drink?'

Gil shook her head. 'No thanks, Aunt Rose. I'm fine.'

'Well, sleep in as long you like in the morning. Dad, Jonas – hot drinks for you?'

Jonas muttered something about being tired himself, and Alan also shook his head. 'No, I think I'll turn in, too.'

They said their good nights, and it was all Gil could do not to run upstairs to her gable room. Her pulse was racing with excitement (but *why*? She still didn't know) and she hurried to the window ledge, where she sat down and peered out at the garden. There were squares of light on the grass, reflecting from the downstairs windows; after a few minutes, though, they went out and everything was in darkness. Gil switched her own lamp off and tried to see through the dark. *Something* was there, she knew it in her bones. Something exciting. Something she must do. If only she could remember . . .

An hour passed, and still she sat gazing out. The sky was clearer tonight, and the moon had risen above the trees, so that the garden was lit by a faint, pearly glow. Then, near the broken-down gate at the end of the garden, a shadow appeared. It began to grow, creeping across the grass like a long finger; then its shape started to change, forming shoulders, a strangely pointed head, like the shadow of someone wearing an ancient headdress . . .

Gil smiled. She stood up, let the curtain fall, and without turning the light on felt for her jacket. Nights were chilly at this time of year. She slipped the jacket on, then moved quietly to the door. No lights on the landing below. Everyone must be asleep by now. *Good*.

Her soft-soled shoes made no sound as, with no conscious awareness of what she was doing, she tiptoed towards the stairs.

Jonas had almost given up when he saw the back door open a crack and Gil emerge. He had nearly fallen asleep several times, and had been on the edge of telling himself that what he suspected wasn't going to happen. Now though, he was thankful that he had decided to wait just a little longer.

He shifted himself behind the curtain of the darkened study window and watched as Gil crossed the garden towards the gate. She didn't look furtive. In fact, he thought, there was a peculiar confidence in the way she walked, as if she knew exactly what she was doing and didn't care who saw her. Jonas didn't believe that for one moment.

He stayed where he was until she had nearly reached the gate, then he darted out of the study and to the kitchen. When he went outside she had vanished, but he dared not risk her seeing him, so he made his way quickly along the wall of the house and down the edge of the garden, where the hedge would hide him. He wondered for a panicky moment if he had left it too late and she was already far enough ahead to give him the slip. But when he got to the gate and peered cautiously over it, he saw her walking away along the lane. And it didn't take a mastermind to guess where she was going.

Jonas started to follow, keeping a safe distance in case Gil should look back over her shoulder. She didn't. She just kept walking with that sense of confident purpose. *Why?* Jonas asked himself. *What's she trying to do?* But his mind couldn't come up with an answer that made any sense.

He gave silent thanks that he had listened to his intuition. It had been obvious all day that something was very wrong with Gil, but the sensible reasoning was that she was simply over-stressed because of all that had happened to her in the last few days. Jonas had thought differently. Perhaps he was getting to know Gil better than either of them had realised, but he had been certain that she was planning something, and when she was so restless this evening it had been easy to put two and two together and work out that whatever it was, she meant to do it tonight. So when everyone else went upstairs he had sneaked back to the study and waited – and the guess had paid off.

Gil was pretty close to the ruined church by now, and she had slowed down. Suddenly she stopped altogether, and hastily Jonas sidestepped and dropped to a crouch in the roadside undergrowth. Gil seemed to be looking around for something. For a few moments nothing happened – then Jonas's breath caught sharply in his throat as two small figures appeared from the darkness. He couldn't see them clearly at this distance, but in the glimmering moonlight he made out the colour of their hair. Red hair . . . *the children* . . .

His heart thumped so hard that he thought he was going to choke. The taller child – *the boy, it must be; he was older* – took hold of Gil's hand and pulled gently. Gil didn't resist but went with him, and the other child, the girl, tagged along behind as they set off again. Jonas waited half a minute, to be safe, then followed.

Any doubt he might have had about where Gil and the children were going vanished when they turned on to the short path that led to old St. Osyth's. He reached the ruined lych gate just in time to see them disappearing into the church, and again he waited, watching to see if anything would happen. Nothing did. No movement, no sound, no sign of life at all.

Or was there . . .? The moon vanished for a moment as some cloud drifted across it, but one faintly glowing patch of light didn't fade with the rest. Jonas tensed. The glow was still there, flickering like candlelight. And it was coming from inside the church.

At this moment Jonas would have given a great deal to have someone else with him. He didn't want to go into the church, because the night was dark and the atmosphere felt dangerous and he was certain that something was in there, waiting. He hadn't even brought a torch, which had to be the dumbest thing of all. How long would it take him to run back to April House and fetch one? Ten minutes? Fifteen? No; that wasn't an option; anything could happen to Gil in that time. *No torch, and no one to help. So it's all down to me . . .*

He was still dithering when from inside the ruin came a strange cry.

Jonas started with shock. He had never heard a sound like that before; it was like a sob and a wail of pain and something else as well – and it jolted him out of his dilemma. Never mind helpers or torches; there wasn't time. Gil was in trouble!

He didn't let himself stop to think about the consequences, but pelted to the church and ran inside.

At first he couldn't see a thing. The moon had been covered by cloud again and the ruin's interior seemed to be one huge block of charcoal shadow. Then suddenly there was another noise, like a soft, low moan. Jonas hastened towards it—

'*Go away!*'

The shout echoed through the ruin, and he recoiled backwards as the red-haired girl leaped from the darkness to bar his way. Her hands were outstretched, palms towards him as if to ward him off, and as the moon came out again he saw her eyes alight with fear.

'Go!' she cried. 'We don't want you here! Run away! *Run!*'

'Elaine!' Suddenly the red-haired boy was there too, grabbing the girl's arm and shaking her into silence. 'I will deal with this!' He swung to face Jonas. 'What do you want?'

'Where's Gil?' Jonas demanded.

'She is here.'

'Where? Take me to her. I—'

'No.' As Jonas tried to push past him, the boy extended one arm and put a hand against his chest. Jonas felt as if someone had pressed a bag of ice-cubes to his heart, and he stumbled back a pace, staring at the boy in horror.

'Go away.' The boy repeated what his sister had said. 'This need not have anything to do with you. Go, while you can.'

'What do you mean? *Where's Gil?*'

'You can't help her,' said the boy flatly. 'Not now. You left it too late. For the last time, *go*, before—'

He stopped abruptly and flung a look back over his shoulder, as if he had heard something that Jonas's ears couldn't pick up. Jonas stared into the dark . . .

And saw a long, gliding shadow moving towards him.

'What is this?' The voice was sweet; almost musical, and it seemed to bypass his hearing and slide straight into his skull. 'Another? Ohh . . . yes, it is.' She was tall and grey and dressed in strange clothes, and at the sight of her Jonas found suddenly that he couldn't move. Her stare hypnotised him. He wanted to say something, but words would not come . . .

The grey woman looked at the younger boy and girl, and smiled. 'What dear children,' she said. 'What good children, to have found another like her.' She turned to Jonas once more. 'Come, my young squire. You want to find Gillian, don't you? She isn't far away. Let me take you to her.'

Jonas's mind spun with confusion. *Young squire?* Who *was* she? Was she real, or – or—

'Come with me to Gillian,' the woman cajoled, and before he realised it Jonas took a step towards her. He saw the red-haired boy mouth two silent words, which looked like, *You fool!* But he couldn't respond. He couldn't do anything at all, except walk slowly after the tall grey figure as she led him into the depths of the church. Something showed in the gloom ahead; a solid block of stone that he recognised as the worn old tomb of Sir Robert and Lady Leece. He didn't want to approach it. But he couldn't stop himself.

Then he saw Gil. She was lying on the floor beside the tomb, huddled up with her head pillowed on her hands. There was a strange smile on her face and at first he thought she was asleep. But as he drew closer she said in a sleepy, almost drawling voice,

'Hello, Jonas. I'm glad you're here, too.'

Jonas looked down at her in bewilderment. Just as Gil had done on the previous night, a part of him was fighting frantically against the trance-like stupor into which his mind was slipping. He *knew* that something about this was horribly wrong. But whenever he tried to work out what it was, it slid away out of his reach, and a voice in his head seemed to whisper, *It's all right, this is how it should be; just give in . . .*

'Gil, I . . .' But he couldn't remember what he had wanted to say. The two children had followed, and now they came to stand by Gil, the boy at her head and the girl at her feet. They gazed solemnly at her but they did not speak.

'There, my dear.' The musical voice flowed over Jonas again. 'You see? Gillian is calm. Let me calm you, too. Let me soothe away your fears and make you happy . . .'

Dreamily, Jonas shuffled around until he was facing her. He was quite tall, but she seemed to tower over him, and the moon cast her shadow across his face and body.

'Be comforted,' she crooned.

Jonas's struggling reason said, *I don't want her comfort—*

'Don't be afraid of me. There's nothing to be afraid of.'

But there is—

'There, now. There, now. Let me stroke your hair. Such a colour . . . Such life . . .'

Why does Gil look so pale? I don't—

The grey woman leaned towards him, and a hand that

felt like a cold cobweb touched his forehead, then his cheek. Unnaturally long fingers stroked downwards until they reached his neck—

A banshee shriek rang through the church and she sprang back like a spring recoiling. Jonas felt a burning sensation in his neck; instinctively his hand went to his throat, and closed round the old leather pouch on its thong.

Instantly the spell on him shattered, and sanity came back in a massive rush. The two children were frozen, staring at him in horror; he didn't pause but let out a ferocious yell that sent them running and scattering; then he whirled and grabbed hold of Gil's arms.

'Gil, get up! We're getting out! *Gil!*'

She said, 'Unhh . . . mmh . . .' and shook her head.

'*Move*, blast you!' Jonas screamed. As the echoes of his scream died away there was a terrible, ominous silence in the church. He snatched a single moment to look around. The children and the grey woman had vanished. But they weren't far away; he would bet anything on that . . .

'Come on, Gil, come on!' Whatever it took, whatever he had to do, he was going to get Gil out of this place! Summoning all his strength he heaved her unceremoniously to her feet and pulled. She stumbled after him, but then started to resist, pulling in the opposite direction.

In Jonas's head a voice whispered, '*Come to me . . .*'

'No!' Jonas shouted, and clamped one hand on the leather pouch again. The voice in his head winked out. But Gil could hear it, he knew she could, for she was smiling and her eyes were glazing over—

He braced himself to do it, and slapped her face, hard. She jolted in shock; her eyes snapped wide open and her mouth opened too. 'Jonas—'

'*Run!*' he snarled, and went, dragging her with him before the evil influence could regain its hold and make her fight him. The moon shone through broken window frames, making shadows leap and cavort around them as they made for the doorway, and at any moment Jonas expected one of the shadows to turn into the grey woman and spring at them. They burst outside, but by this time Gil was starting to protest and it was all he could do to drag her across the overgrown graveyard to the lych gate.

'Gil, stop it! Stop fighting me!' Maybe the influence would be weaker once they were clear of the church. Praying that it would, he shoved her forcibly through the gate ahead of him, and just managed to stop her from falling to her hands and knees on the path. *Move, move, move!* But though she did not want to move, she wasn't resisting any more; she was suddenly like a rag doll, with no will of her own.

'Right,' Jonas said with grim determination. 'Let's get you home!' *Though if anything follows us, I don't know what the hell I'll be able to do about it . . .*

140

The lane was empty, the night almost eerily peaceful. But getting Gil home wasn't going to be easy. She now felt more like a sack of potatoes than a rag doll; she leaned on Jonas, her feet dragging and her head and arms flopping, and his own arms were soon aching fierily with the effort of supporting her limp weight. He kept looking back the way they had come, dreading that he might see a grey phantom gliding along the road after them. Nothing came, but all the same Jonas struggled on as fast as he could, wondering with each panting, fearful breath if his strength would hold out until they reached home.

They were almost at a bend in the lane when it happened. Jonas had looked backwards yet again, at the same time heaving Gil more securely into his arms. As he turned to face forward once more, a tall, dark shadow formed from the darkness and towered into his path.

Jonas's heart gave a colossal lurch and his entire body seemed to turn to jelly. Gil fell from his grasp, slumping on to the road, but he couldn't help her; all his brain could register was a surge of horror and blind panic. He stumbled backwards, hands flailing, opened his mouth to scream with all the power he possessed—

A voice said, '*Jonas!*' and the scream stuck in his throat before he could utter it. Shaking and shuddering, his face dead-white and eyes bulging in shock, Jonas stared at the apparition looming before him, and croaked,

'*Granfa . . . ?*'

11

It took all Jonas's remaining energy to keep up with Alan Granger's cracking pace as he strode back to April House with Gil in his arms. Stumbling across the garden in his grandfather's wake, he didn't know whether he wanted to laugh hysterically, cry, or just fall down where he was and sleep until this whole insane scenario went away.

Neither of them had the breath to say much as they went in at the back door. Alan hissed, 'Study. Switch the light on.'

Jonas obeyed like a robot, running ahead as Alan carried Gil's limp form across the hall and into the study. He laid her on the couch at one side of the room. She didn't stir when he touched her; her eyes were closed and when he lifted one of her eyelids all he saw was the white.

'God almighty . . .' Alan said through clenched teeth. He swung to face Jonas. 'What happened?'

Jonas swallowed. 'She went . . .' He faltered.

'Where?' Alan's eyes narrowed. 'The old church?'

'How did you—'

'Never mind! Just tell me everything you can, *quickly*!'

Jonas's nerves were so strained that he felt as if

something inside his head was about to burst. 'There was . . . I saw . . .' But the attempt to explain collapsed and he shook his head violently.

'What? *What* did you see?'

'You wouldn't believe me!'

'Try me! For God's sake, boy, whether it's believable or not, there isn't time for dithering!'

Any thought Jonas might have made about hiding the truth collapsed as he saw the look of dread on his grandfather's face. In disjointed sentences he told Alan how he had followed Gil to the ruined church, and what had taken place there. His voice started to shake as he described the two red-haired children – and when he reached the point where the grey phantom had appeared, his nerve deserted him.

'I can't,' he whispered. 'I just c–can't *talk* about it . . .' He shut his eyes, covering his face with one hand.

Alan said quietly, 'A woman, very tall, wearing mediaeval dress. Everything about her grey. Was that what you saw?'

Jonas's hand dropped and his face beneath it was deathly pale. 'You know?'

Alan nodded. 'I've seen her myself, and I know who – and what – she is. Jonas, this is vital – did that thing physically touch either of you?'

'I – I don't know about Gil,' Jonas said in confusion. 'When I found her she was just lying there . . .'

'And you? For all our sakes, Jonas, tell me!'

Long, icy fingers on his face, moving down to his neck . . .
Then a howling shriek, a sense of burning, and the phantom
had vanished as reason came smashing back into his mind . . .
Jonas shut his eyes again and nodded. 'But something s–
stopped it. I don't know; it was as if—'

'Wait.' Alan's eyes narrowed. He reached out, caught
hold of the thong around Jonas's neck, and with a quick
jerk pulled out the leather pouch.

'The charm worked,' he said softly. 'It repelled her . . .'
Then he examined the pouch more closely. 'What's this
mark on it?'

'Mark?' Jonas echoed dazedly.

'Like a burn.'

He looked. Imprinted on the leather of the pouch
was a clear, dark scorch. It was in the shape of a
thumbprint.

His skin crawled, but before he could say any of the
things that were crowding in his brain Alan strode across
the room to a tall cupboard that stood in one corner.
Taking a key from his pocket he unlocked the cupboard
door and took out a glass jar with a screw top, and
another small pouch like the one Jonas wore. The jar was
filled with what looked like dried herbs; a strong smell
came from it as Alan took off the lid, and he shook some
of the contents into the pouch.

'String,' he snapped to Jonas. And as Jonas looked
blank, 'In the kitchen – cut me about a metre. Hurry
up!'

As he ran to the kitchen, Jonas was hoping against hope that in a moment he would wake up and find that none of this was real. He felt detached, numb, disbelieving . . . He found the string and took a length of it to the study, where Alan threaded the pouch on to it and sat down beside Gil. As he looped the charm around her neck she sighed and her eyelids fluttered, but she didn't wake.

'Granfa,' Jonas said fearfully, 'will she be all right?'

'I think so, yes; at least in the short term. But something's begun, and I just hope to heaven it isn't too late.'

'Wh . . . what do you mean?' Then suddenly Jonas's self-control snapped under a surge of fear and bewilderment. His voice rose to a shout. 'You've known for years, haven't you? You know what this thing is – it got Gil's sister, and now it's got Gil, too! *Why didn't you tell me?*'

'Be quiet!' his grandfather hissed. 'You'll wake your mother!'

Jonas was too angry and frightened to care. 'So what if I do?' he fired back. 'Maybe you ought to have the guts to tell her, too!'

'He did, love,' said Rose's voice from the door.

Neither of them had heard her approach, but she was in the doorway in her dressing gown. Her face was pale and there was a dark shadow under her visible eye.

'He told me when you were first born,' she said, 'as soon as he found out that you had red hair. It's why he

145

didn't want us to come and live here after your dad left. And why he never let your Aunt Jean bring Gil and Biddy to visit.'

'Red hair.' Jonas was still staring at his grandfather. 'That's the link, isn't it?'

'Yes,' said Rose. 'Any red-headed child living in Neapham is in danger – and has been for centuries.' She came in, closing the door behind her. 'I didn't believe the story to start with. But I changed my mind.'

'When?' Jonas demanded.

She smiled sadly. 'Remember, when you were younger, you told us about the two red-haired children you'd seen near the beach, and you asked who they were? And then there was that shadow that came across the garden towards your bedroom.'

Jonas's jaw tightened. 'I remember.'

'Well, your granfa and I both saw it, too.'

Jonas shot a furious look at Alan. 'You said I'd imagined it all! The kids weren't really there and the shadow was just a bad dream – you lied to me!'

'He didn't want you to be frightened, love,' said Rose, trying to soothe. 'Neither of us did.'

'Oh, great!' Jonas exploded. 'So instead you left me to find out the hard way, is that it?'

'You were protected,' Alan said. 'Your mother and I made sure of that. If Gil's family hadn't come to Neapham, nothing would have happened and you need never have known.'

'But they *did* come!' Jonas turned on his heel, pointing at the couch. 'And now Gil's unconscious, and her little sister's in hospital, and I can't believe that I saw what I did . . .' He sucked in a huge breath. 'Mum, Granfa – you've got to level with me. *What's going on in the church?*'

Rose said: 'It's gone too far now, Dad. He's got a right to know.'

'Yes,' Alan said. 'He has. I'm sorry, Jonas. I was wrong not to level with you, as you put it. And I made another terrible mistake tonight.' He pinched the bridge of his nose, looking suddenly worn out. 'I knew there was something wrong with Gil. Her peculiar mood, her tiredness, the way she suddenly became so secretive . . . it all fitted the picture. I expected her to go to the church tonight, so I waited up. I was going to follow her, and try to . . . well, whatever I was going to try to do, I failed, because I fell asleep.' He gave a bitter little smile. 'Blame it on my age. I haven't got the stamina for late nights any more. But if I could turn the clock back a few hours—'

He stopped in mid-sentence as Gil groaned and opened her eyes.

'Gil!' Forgetting everything else, Jonas ran to the couch. 'Gil, it's me, it's Jonas! Can you see me, Gil? Can you hear me?'

Gil said, in a weak voice that didn't sound like her own, 'Feel sick . . .' Then with no warning she leaned over and threw up on the floor.

'Ohh . . .' she moaned. 'I'm sorry . . . sorry . . .'

'Don't worry; I'll clear it.' Ever practical, Rose hurried to the kitchen for a bowl of water and a cloth. By the time she came back Alan had pushed Jonas aside and was crouching beside Gil.

'It's all right,' he said gently. 'You've had a little accident, but it's nothing to worry about.'

'Can't . . . remember,' Gil whispered.

'That's probably just as well.' Alan darted a look at Jonas, silently warning him not to say anything. Rose cleaned up the mess, then straightened. 'I think we'd better get her upstairs to bed, Dad.'

'Yes. You know what to do about . . . everything else?'

Jonas didn't understand that cryptic question, but his mother nodded and hurried out with the bowl. A few moments later Jonas heard her feet on the stairs.

'My wrist still hurts,' Gil said hazily. 'And my neck . . . Did the brambles scratch me again?'

'Brambles?' Alan echoed. 'What brambles?'

'At the church. When we went there before . . .'

Shocked, Alan turned on Jonas. 'You went to that place with her before last night?'

He had left out that part of the story. 'Yes,' he admitted miserably. 'She'd found something; she wanted to show it to me—'

'Never mind; never mind! Tell me about the brambles.'

Jonas told him. 'She put a plaster on it when we got back.' He glanced at Gil's arm. 'There, look.'

Alan carefully peeled the sticking plaster away. The

148

marks of the scratches were still clear, and the skin around them was red and angry.

'Hurts,' Gil said. '*Stings.*'

'So that's how it started,' Alan said softly. He looked hard at Gil. 'You said your neck hurts, too. Where, Gil?'

She put up a hand and fumbled vaguely. Peering, Jonas saw to his shock that there were more marks at her throat. They looked just like the scratches on her wrist. Just like the marks of long, sharp nails . . .

'Granfa, what *are* they?' he asked urgently. But Alan only shook his head and wouldn't answer. Then Rose came back.

'Everything's ready,' she said.

'Good.' Alan stood up. 'Now, Gil, we're going to take you up to your room. You can have a good night's sleep, and you'll feel better in the morning. All right?'

'Mmm . . . all right, Uncle Alan . . .' Her head lolled as he gathered her up, and, telling Jonas to wait where he was, he carried her out with Rose at his heels.

Left alone in the study, Jonas paced restlessly, trying to control the explosive mixture of worry and anger and fear. He wanted to think clearly but it was impossible, and his mind was still whirling when his mother and grandfather returned.

'How's Gil?' Jonas demanded.

'She's fine,' said Rose soothingly. 'Your granfa's given her something to help her sleep.'

Jonas nodded. 'So,' he said to Alan. 'Your turn to tell a story.'

'Yes . . . You'd better sit down. Rose, could you make us all some coffee?'

'Of course.' Rose went out again, and there was silence for a few moments. Jonas had sat down but he was restless, fidgety. Then Alan started to speak.

'The creature you saw in the church – the grey woman – isn't human,' he said. 'Not any more. She was, once; but now, she's . . . well, the nearest explanation I can give you is that she's a kind of . . . vampire.'

'That's crazy!' Jonas whispered. 'Vampires are horror movie stuff, not real!'

'Oh, this one's real,' said Alan grimly. 'But not in the way you think. This isn't a Dracula story, with coffins and garlic and stakes through the heart. It's much more subtle, and much more dangerous. Because, if my theory's right, what she feeds on – and thrives on – is life energy. She doesn't do any real physical damage; that's not how it works. She takes over her victims' minds, then saps their strength until there's nothing left, and they die.'

Jonas shuddered. 'You said she was human, once. Who *was* she?'

'I can't be absolutely certain,' said Alan. 'But the evidence, with the history I've pieced together over the years, fits all too well. That creature has been dead for more than seven hundred years. But when she was alive, her name was Joanna Leece.'

'The Leeces were the most important family around here in early mediaeval times,' Alan said. 'The first one, Humphrey, came over with the Norman invasion, and King William gave him the land as a reward for helping in the Conquest. They were called de Lys then, but it got Anglicised later . . . however, it's not Humphrey who concerns us.'

'It's Robert,' said Jonas.

His grandfather looked keenly at him. 'Of course; you've already been doing some sleuthing, haven't you? You've seen Robert's tomb.'

'And Joanna's.'

'Yes, Joanna's . . . She was Robert's second wife. His first wife died very young.'

'How?' Jonas asked.

'Oh, nothing suspicious. It was probably in childbirth; that was very common in those days. Anyway, after Elaine died—'

Jonas frowned as a memory triggered. 'Elaine . . . The red-haired girl – that's *her* name!'

'Are you sure?'

'Yes. I heard the boy say it. They're brother and sister.'

'Then they must be Sir Robert's children,' Alan breathed. 'It's all starting to fit . . .'

'Fit what?' Jonas asked nervously. 'You mean, the children are ghosts? As old as that . . . that *thing*?'

'They're ghosts, yes,' said Alan. 'And they've been haunting the church for centuries. You see, Joanna murdered them.'

As Jonas digested this, he reached into a bookshelf and brought out a small book with a plain leather cover. The edges were worn and the pages yellow and speckled with age; if there had ever been a title on the cover, it had faded to nothing.

'This book was written by a historian in the eighteenth century,' said Alan. 'It wasn't published, because what it has to say would have upset too many people, especially the church authorities. But the historian did a lot of research. He came up with a theory about the Leeces, and he had the book printed privately.' His eyes looked very dark. 'The story he tells is very hard to believe. But I believe it.'

The basics of the story as Alan told it were straightforward enough. A few years after his first wife died, Sir Robert Leece met Joanna. He was a very wealthy man, and Joanna was ambitious; she set out to snare him, he was dazzled by her beauty and they were married. But Joanna was jealous of Robert's children from his first marriage. He loved them very much – more, she thought, than he loved her – and she feared that, once she began to age and lose her looks, her husband would no longer want her. So she turned to the powers of darkness.

Rose, who had brought a pot of strong coffee and

three mugs on a tray, saw Jonas's sceptical face and said, 'I know it sounds like superstitious nonsense, but remember, in those days people firmly believed in evil forces. For someone to "sell their soul to the devil" was perfectly logical to their way of thinking.'

Alan continued with the story. Some time later Sir Robert went away to war. He was gone a year – and while he was away, Joanna killed both the children. When her husband returned she tried to pretend that they had died of a fever, but one of Sir Robert's servants had spied on her and knew the truth.

'According to an ancient document, it was discovered that: "she with their blood and bones did perform devilish sorcery, that she might gain unto herself the virtues of their innocent and youthful spirits",' Alan quoted. His face grew grim. 'She believed that by sacrificing the children she would stay young and beautiful, and keep her husband. But the servant told his master what he had seen, and under torture, Joanna confessed.'

'That's *sick*,' Jonas said with a shudder. 'Sorcery and murder, and then torture to make her tell . . . what sort of people *were* they?'

'Perfectly normal, by their standards,' Alan reminded him. 'Joanna should have been put on trial for witchcraft. But Sir Robert knew that the scandal was likely to ruin him. So he and the local priest decided on her punishment, and they carried it out with the help of those villagers who could be trusted not to tell the outside world. She was burned alive, and her ashes walled up in the church.'

Rose shuddered, and Jonas pulled a revolted face. 'Then the tomb—'

'Doesn't contain her remains, and never did. When Sir Robert died a few years later, the locals had a memorial made to them both, so that no one would be suspicious. They thought that would be the end of the story – but it wasn't. Because Joanna's evil spirit came back.'

Not long after Sir Robert's death, the document went on, rumour began that St. Osyth's was haunted. People described encounters with a tall woman dressed in grey, and some also saw two red-haired children in the vicinity of the church. The priest, and the villagers who knew about the crime and execution, realised that Joanna and her victims had come back.

Then several village children fell ill. The sickness was a mystery; nothing could be done for them, and they faded and died, as if the life force had been drained from them. Every one was red-haired. The attacks grew worse and worse, and no amount of exorcism made any difference; until at last the locals became so afraid of Joanna that they abandoned their church, leaving it to rot and building another, identical church next to it.

'The "new" church has never suffered from hauntings,' said Alan. 'But Joanna Leece still haunts the old one. And any young, red-haired person who comes to Neapham is a potential new victim. As we all know to our cost.'

He shut the book, and for nearly a minute there was silence except for the tick of a clock on the mantelpiece. Then Jonas let out his breath in a long whistle.

'It *is* a crazy story,' he said. 'But I believe it. After what I saw last night, I haven't got much choice, have I?' He took a swig of coffee; it had gone cold but he didn't notice. 'Granfa, what are we going to do? There's got to be some way to help Gil and Biddy!'

'I think there is,' said Alan, 'but it won't be easy. In fact, it could be downright dangerous.'

'Who for?'

'All of us. But chiefly Gil.'

Jonas hunched his shoulders. 'Seems to me she's in danger already. What's a bit more?' His fists clenched. '*Why* did you make her stay here when her mum and dad left? If she'd gone with them, nothing would have happened to her!'

'I didn't want her to stay,' said Alan. 'But by the time Biddy was moved to London, it was too late. Joanna had already found her.'

'The shadow in the garden—'

'Yes. Joanna came looking for Gil on her first night here. Biddy must have been the link. And once the link is made, it doesn't matter how far away the victim travels; Joanna's power will reach out.'

'So taking Biddy away made no difference?'

'That's right. And it would have made no difference to Gil, either. Distance buys some more time, but in the end the result is the same. Joanna will take all the life energy they have, until there's nothing left.'

Jonas stared at him. 'Are you saying they'll both . . . die?'

'Yes,' said Alan. 'I'm afraid they will.'

12

They all went to bed soon afterwards. Jonas felt almost drunk with tiredness, but as his grandfather disappeared up the stairs he turned to Rose. 'Mum, why didn't you tell me about Joanna before?'

Rose sighed. 'We truly didn't think there was any need. The pouch your granfa made for you protected you – just the way it did tonight. The only other redheads in the family were Gil and Biddy, and Granfa made sure that they didn't come here.' Her mouth gave an odd, sad twist. 'Your Aunt Jean never liked him much, so she wasn't keen to visit anyway. So we thought everything would be all right, and it would never happen again.'

A quick frown creased Jonas's face. 'What do you mean, "again"?' he asked.

Rose realised she had slipped up and tried to cover it. 'Oh – nothing; it—'

'Mum, has something like this happened before? *Please*, Mum, if it has, you've got to tell me!'

Rose bit her lip. But she couldn't deny it now. 'It was long before I was born,' she said quietly. 'More than fifty years ago, in fact. But your granfa told me about it when I brought you to live here after Dad left. You see . . . that thing in the old church killed his brother.'

Jonas's eyes widened. He tried to say something, but couldn't find any words.

'His name was George, and he was about three years younger than you when he died,' Rose went on. 'Your granfa was involved somehow; I don't know all the details, because he's never told me. But it's what made him believe in the story of Joanna.'

One death in the family, Jonas thought. And if something wasn't done, there would be more . . . 'He said we weren't to tell Gil,' he said. 'But that isn't fair, Mum! She's the one who's in danger – she's got a right to know!'

'Granfa's only thinking of her, love.' She glanced sidelong at him. 'I know it doesn't seem like it sometimes, but he loves all his family, and he won't let anything happen if he can possibly stop it. Trust him.' She kissed his cheek. 'Please, Jonas. Go to bed now. And try to sleep.'

Jonas didn't have the heart to argue with her. They didn't speak again as they switched the lights off and went up the stairs. Jonas started towards the west gable – but as soon as Rose was out of sight he turned instead towards the east gable and Gil's room. He needed to see her. If she was awake, he needed to talk.

A faint light showed under Gil's bedroom door. Jonas turned the handle, eased the door open, looked in . . . and stopped still.

A single shaded lamp was on, and by its soft glow he saw Gil lying in bed. The pouch on its length of string was still round her neck. And something else had been hung up at the window: a garland of dried leaves and flowers and grasses, like a Hawaiian lei. Even from the doorway he could smell them; a heavy, oppressive scent that made his nostrils curl. Then he looked at the floor and saw that someone had sprinkled more dried herbs on the carpet, making a circle around the bed.

For some time Jonas stood motionless, gazing at the room with a growing sense of dread. Gil was asleep – he could hear the regular rhythm of her breathing – and all his ideas about waking her and talking collapsed. Granfa and Mum had done this for a reason. He couldn't disturb it. He *dared* not.

He closed the door very, very quietly, and went away to the west gable and the sanctuary of his own room.

The phone at April House had a penetratingly loud bell, and at seven o'clock it woke everyone except Gil.

Though he was thick-headed with tiredness, Jonas knew that such an early call must mean something important. He thought instantly of Biddy, and with a growing sense of alarm stumbled out of his room. The bell stopped shrilling as he came down the west gable stairs, and he saw his grandfather picking up the extension on the main landing.

'Tony – is everything all right?'

Tony – Gil's dad – Jonas stopped still, listening, and Rose came hurrying along the landing from her own room. What they heard told them nothing; Gil's father was doing most of the talking, with Alan only putting in an occasional word. Eventually Alan just said, 'Right, yes. I understand, of course. I think so too. All right, Tony. Thanks very much for letting me know. No, I won't say a word to her; rely on it. Give our love to Jean. And try not to worry too much. Bye.'

He put the receiver down, his face serious, and Jonas said, 'What's happened?'

'Is Gil awake? Alan asked.

'She can't be.' Rose glanced in the direction of the east gable. 'If the bell had woken her, she'd have been here by now.'

'Good. Because she mustn't know about this. During the night, Biddy woke up.'

Jonas's face lit. 'She's come round?'

'No. That's the alarming part of it. Gil's dad was with her when it happened – thank God her mum wasn't, so she didn't see – but Biddy sat up, opened her eyes, looked straight across the room, and laughed. Then she fell back unconscious again.'

'*What? That's weird.*'

'I'm afraid it might be more than weird,' said Alan. 'I think it's a sign that Joanna's influence is getting stronger. She has a link with Gil, too, now; and Gil and Biddy are sisters. So what affects one might well affect the other.'

'Do Gil's mum and dad know about Joanna?' Jonas demanded.

'Up to a point. They know the legend that red-haired children are in danger; but of course they don't believe it.'

'Don't they?' asked Rose. 'Even now?'

He sighed. 'They're very "sensible" people. And Jean in particular is as stubborn as a mule, with a temper to match. Even if the evidence is staring them in the face, they don't *want* to believe it.'

'But you frightened them into letting Gil stay.'

'Yes . . . I suppose there was just enough doubt in their minds . . . and of course it was a way out of a problem, because Gil couldn't have stayed at the hospital with them, and she's too young to be on her own at home.' He started to pace up and down the hall. 'If only I could persuade them to protect Biddy, the way Jonas – and Gil, now – have been protected!'

'Isn't it too late for that?' Rose asked.

'It would buy us more time, and that might make all the difference.'

'Time for what?' Jonas demanded. 'Granfa – last night, you said you thought there was a way to save Gil and Biddy, but it was dangerous. What would we have to do?'

Alan hesitated and seemed to be debating what to say. Then he decided. 'There's no point telling you all the details; better to show you when – if – the time comes. But it would mean using someone as bait to lure Joanna into the open. And the only suitable candidate is Gil.'

No wonder he said it was dangerous! Jonas thought, and protested, 'There's got to be another way! Why can't I be the bait?'

'Because of what happened at the church last night,' said Alan. 'Joanna tried to snare you and, quite literally, got her fingers burned. She won't dare try again.'

Jonas fingered the pouch at his neck uncertainly. 'My talisman hurt her?'

'Oh, yes. I'm convinced that it, and certain other things like the garlands, are the key to defeating her. Possibly to destroying her completely. But it'll take time to prepare everything I need. And after what we've just heard on the phone, I know that time is running out. If we could only protect Biddy—'

'Couldn't you persuade Jean and Tony, Dad?' Rose asked urgently. 'If you told them about Gil—'

'Tony would get straight in his car and drive up here to take her away, and that would be the worst thing of all. No: they *mustn't* know. I can try to persuade them to take what steps they can to protect Biddy. But I daren't tell them the rest.'

'Then I don't rate your chances of succeeding,' Rose said. 'Knowing Jean, especially.' She paused, suddenly thoughtful. 'Unless you go to London.'

Alan swung round and stared at her. 'What?'

Rose's eyes had an eager light in them. 'If you try to persuade them on the phone, they'll just hang up on you. But if you're face to face, they'll *have* to listen!'

Alan's grim expression began to change. 'You might be right. It could be the one chance . . . Look, I'll get dressed and get the car out. Rose, can you make a flask of tea, and some sandwiches, anything I can eat on the way.'

'Right,' said Rose and ran towards the main stairs. Alan started back to his bedroom and Jonas said, 'Granfa! What can *I* do?'

'Stay here, and make sure Gil does, too,' Alan told him. 'And help your mother. She'll have things to prepare for when I get back.'

Alan left ten minutes later, with last-minute pleas from Rose to drive carefully and, whatever he did, not lose his temper with Gil's mother when he confronted her. He had borrowed Jonas's mobile phone and promised to ring as soon as there was any news. For his part, Jonas had promised not to tell Gil anything of what was going on; he had been reluctant, but Alan insisted it was the safest way. As the car disappeared down the drive, Jonas shut the door and went into the kitchen, where Rose was rummaging through a cupboard.

'What are you looking for?' he asked. He felt strangely flat, yet nervy at the same time. It was very unsettling.

'Something I thought I had . . . some herbs.' Rose straightened, pushing her hair out of her eyes. 'Must've run out. Look, Jonas, as soon as the shops open I'm going to have to drive into town and get a few things. If Gil wakes up before I get back, make sure she stays around the house, all right?'

'All right.' He looked up at the ceiling, as if he could see through it to the upper floors. 'I wish I could tell her.'

'Please, love, remember what Granfa said – it's too dangerous! We can't predict how she'd react; she might go and do something stupid. Granfa will be back by this evening, so we'll see what he says then.' She looked searchingly at him. 'Don't tell her. Promise me.'

'OK,' Jonas agreed with a sigh. 'I promise.'

Rose had been gone an hour by the time Gil came downstairs. Her clothes were crumpled, her hair looked like a badly clipped hedge, and there were heavy shadows under her eyes.

'Where is everyone?' she said as she came yawning into the kitchen and found only Jonas. 'Have I missed breakfast?'

' 'Fraid so.' Jonas tried to sound casual but suspected it wasn't too convincing.

'Oh.' Another yawn. 'That's a relief.'

He pretended to laugh. 'How are you feeling?'

'Fine. Well – tired, and a bit achy, now you ask, but . . . Why are you staring at me like that?'

'I'm not,' he said, hastily looking away.

'You were. As if I'd grown another head, or something.'

Jonas put the kettle on, to give himself an excuse to

face the Aga while he tried to calm his nervousness. 'Sorry,' he said lightly. 'I was probably thinking about something else. Want some tea?'

'No, thanks.' She yawned a third time. 'I had some seriously weird dreams last night; that must be why I feel so tired. Can't remember anything about them now, though. Oh – except that I thought I heard the phone, really early. Jonas, did Mum or Dad ring? Is Biddy—'

'No,' Jonas lied, quickly interrupting. 'No one rang; it must have been in your dream.'

'Thank God for that! I wish I could call them . . .'

'They told you not to, didn't they? Because of not using mobile phones in the hospital.'

'Yeah.' She sagged on to the nearest chair and rubbed her eyes. 'So, where are Uncle Alan and Aunt Rose?'

'Mum's gone into town, shopping.' Jonas hesitated, then remembered his promise. 'And Granfa's got another meeting or something. He won't be back till this evening.'

Did he detect an odd glint in Gil's eyes as he said that? Hard to be sure, but he was suddenly alert. Then she said, 'By the way, I've got a bone to pick with someone.'

'Oh? Not me, I hope.'

'It depends on whether it was you who put all those leaves and stuff back in my room.'

Just in time Jonas remembered to play dumb. 'No,' he said. 'It wasn't. It must have been Mum.'

Gil snorted angrily, 'Why does she keep *doing* that?

I *hate* those things – they look revolting, and the smell makes me feel sick. I keep throwing them out; I thought she'd got the message by now, but she obviously hasn't.'

'She's a bit like that,' Jonas said. 'You know – gets bees in her bonnet. She probably thinks they're good for you, or something. I'll have a word with her on the quiet.'

'Good. I didn't even notice them last night, or I'd have said something then. But it's probably better if you do it.' Gil looked down at herself. 'Know what? I went to sleep in my clothes. I *really* must have been out of it.'

'Don't you remember?'

She frowned at him. 'Remember what?'

'Oh . . . Going to bed and things.' He watched her surreptitiously.

'No,' she said, 'funnily enough, I don't. If you asked me what I did for most of the evening, I couldn't tell you. So it can't have been very interesting.' She stood up again. 'I'm going to have a shower. You'll shout for me if anyone rings, won't you?'

'Course,' said Jonas. He was glad she didn't see his face as she went out.

Upstairs again, Gil grabbed her towel and went to the bathroom. She started to undress, then stopped, staring in astonishment as for the first time she saw the pouch on its length of string around her neck.

'*Ugh!*' She grabbed at it and tore it off, holding it at arm's length. Someone must have put it there while she was asleep . . . 'Aunt Rose again!' she said aloud, her teeth clenched furiously. 'How the *hell* did she manage it without waking me? What is going *on*?'

For a moment a memory almost came to her, and it was something hideous and terrible. But then it vanished, and her anger surged back. The bathroom had a small, old-fashioned casement window; Gil thumped it open, and hurled the pouch as far as she could into the garden. She didn't see where it landed, and didn't care; she just slammed the window shut again before starting to run the shower.

Rose returned with several large, lightweight but bulky bags, which she did not want Gil to see. Jonas helped her to take them to a little-used room, and Rose shut herself away with the bags, a ball of twine, scissors and needles and cotton.

'What's she doing?' Gil asked with mild curiosity, seeing Rose's back view as she went into the room and shut the door.

Jonas knew very well what she was doing, but only shrugged and said, 'Search me. She said not to disturb her. Just being Mum, I expect.'

'Well, when she comes out, tell her about those lousy leaves, will you? If I find any more in my room—'

'OK, OK; I said I'd have a word.'

'Right.' Gil was not in a good mood. The stuff in her room was bad enough, but finding the pouch tied round her neck had heightened her temper to a very volatile level. She still felt tired, the scratches on her wrist were sore and her throat hurt. And on top of all that there was an atmosphere in the house; a sense of furtiveness, things being hidden, secrets being kept. Rose was obviously up to something, and Gil felt sure that Jonas was in on the conspiracy. The way he had looked at her first thing this morning had been a giveaway, though he had tried to disguise it. Something was going on, and Gil was determined to find out what it was.

There was no sign of Rose at what would normally be lunchtime. Jonas made himself a cheese sandwich but Gil wasn't hungry. She wandered into the garden, and was not surprised when, a minute later, he followed, plate in hand and still eating. He'd been wandering around barefoot all morning and hadn't even stopped to put some shoes on before coming outside. She was certain now that he was tailing her. Everywhere she went, he turned up by 'coincidence' soon afterwards, and this little test was the final proof. All right; then maybe she would turn the tables.

She said, 'I think I'll go for a walk.'

Jonas's head came up quickly. 'Where?' he asked.

'I don't know. The beach, maybe.' She waited for the expected answer, and got it.

'I'll come with you.'

'There's no need,' she said.

'No, really. I could do with some exercise anyway.'

Gil shrugged in a 'suit yourself' way and set off towards the gate.

'Hey, hang on!' Jonas called after her. 'I haven't finished my sandwich yet!'

She looked over her shoulder. 'Then you can catch me up later. See you!'

Jonas swore under his breath as she strode away. He dashed back to the kitchen, cramming the last of his sandwich into his mouth as he went, dumped his plate in the sink and ran to the room where Rose was working.

'Mum!' He burst in. Rose was listening to the radio with headphones on; she saw him and took them off.

'Gil's gone for a walk, or so she says. I'd better go with her.'

'Right,' said Rose. 'Don't let her go near the old church!'

'I won't. Just get my shoes—'

He went without waiting for an answer, found a pair of battered trainers in the scullery and was pulling them on when the phone rang.

'Damn!' His mother would have the headphones on again and wouldn't hear the bell. Better answer it, just in case . . .

He hopped across the hall with the second shoe half on, and grabbed the receiver. 'Hello?'

'Jonas, is that you?'

'Granfa! What's happened?'

'The worst thing that could,' Alan's voice came down the line. 'The car's broken down – just died on me and won't start again!'

'Oh, no! Where are you?'

'Somewhere near Colchester, I think; though I'm not sure. I've called a breakdown service, but God alone knows how long it'll take them to get here. Look, Jonas, if it takes too long, or they can't fix it, then I won't go on to London. Whatever the case, though, I've no idea what time I'll be back. So I want you to keep a *very* close watch on Gil – particularly after it gets dark. All right?'

'Right, Granfa.'

'Tell your mother what's happened. And if there's any kind of emergency, ring me back.'

'I will. Good luck.'

Jonas hung up. Telling Mum would waste another minute . . . but he couldn't go and leave her in the dark.

Praying that Gil wasn't walking into the ruined church at this very moment, he ran back to Rose.

Gil knew that Jonas would come after her, so the only surprise was how long it took him to do it. She had reached the turning to the beach path before she heard his running footsteps in the lane, but she didn't stop or even slow down as he came racing to catch up.

'You don't have to walk that fast!' he said, gasping.

'I feel like walking fast. Like I said, you don't have to come.'

He didn't answer that but fell into step beside her. They turned in silence through the gap in the pine trees, and a minute later emerged on to the dunes. The sea looked grey and cold under the cloudy sky, and for as far as the eye could see in both directions the beach was deserted.

'Bit different to a sunny day, isn't it?' Jonas said, attempting to make conversation.

'Mm.' Gil stood on a dune top, gazing over the water. Then, taking him completely by surprise, she added, 'OK. What's going on?'

His pulse gave an uncomfortable lurch and he tried to think fast. 'Uh? Sorry, I don't—'

'Yes, you do!' She pivoted to face him, her face angry. 'Don't try to pretend, Jonas; I'm not a complete idiot! The stuff in my room, that stupid bag of herbs that someone put round my neck – and all morning you've been treating me as if I'd just landed from an alien planet!'

'I haven't!' he protested.

'Yes, you have, and don't try to deny it! Asking me if I'm OK, and all this "don't you remember?" business. *What* am I supposed to remember?' She sucked in breath, shaking now with fury. 'I want to know what you and your family are up to, Jonas, so you'd better tell me, *now!*'

Jonas was in a terrible dilemma. Gil wasn't going to be satisfied with an evasive answer, and he didn't think he

171

could lie well enough to convince her that there was nothing wrong. Yet his grandfather had warned him that telling her the truth would mean running a terrible risk . . .

Gil was waiting, getting impatient, and Jonas had to make a decision. 'Look,' he said desperately, 'I don't know where you got this idea from, but there is *nothing* going on!' He swallowed. 'If there was, I'd tell you. Honestly.'

She continued to stare coldly at him for a moment or two. Then she said contemptuously, 'Liar!'

And she turned and ran away along the beach, back in the direction of April House.

'Gil!' Jonas shouted. 'Gil, wait! Come back!' But she ignored him and kept running.

'Oh, hell—' Jonas slithered down the side of the dune, meaning to run after her. He reached the bottom, feet slithering in the soft sand – and a voice said,

'Don't let her come back!'

Shock nearly tipped Jonas off his feet. He spun round—

And came face to face with Elaine.

13

She stood in front of him, small and wide-eyed and piteous. Jonas was stunned. He knew she had appeared to Gil in daylight, but somehow he had never quite believed it was possible. Nor did she look like a ghost; if, indeed, she was a ghost and not something stranger. Everything about her – her bright red hair, the strange clothes she wore, the pleading expression on her face – seemed as real and solid as he was.

He tried to say something but found he couldn't. Elaine reached out towards him; instinctively he flinched away, and he could have sworn that tears brimmed in her eyes. *Can ghosts cry?* he thought.

'Jonas,' she said. 'You are Jonas.'

He found his voice with difficulty. 'Y-yes . . .'

'I know you are Gillian's friend. You must help her. You must not let her come back.'

'Back . . . where?' Jonas managed to get out.

She looked over her shoulder and her voice dropped to a frightened whisper. 'To the church. *She* will call her. *She* will be waiting. I pray you, Jonas, don't let her come!'

Jonas didn't know whether he was frightened or angry or both. 'But *you* came for her!' he said. 'In the garden. You *lured* her!'

'I had no choice,' Elaine replied. 'It is what we must do, Edmund and I. *She* wills it, and we must obey her. But it is not what we desire.'

'You mean . . . she controls you?'

Elaine's look gave him his answer, and Jonas believed her. She could have been lying, but gut instinct told him she was not. She wanted to help Gil. Otherwise, why would she have appeared to him, perhaps risking Joanna's fury, and say what she had?

He was about to ask her another question when there was a disturbance in the tall marram grass, and Jonas turned his head in time to see the boy, Edmund, appear from behind the dune. Wrathfully he confronted his sister and hissed, '*What have you done?*'

She shrank back but her voice was defiant. 'I want to help Gillian!'

'You can't help her!' Edmund snapped. 'You know what we must do! Come, now; come away – obey me!'

Elaine's lower lip trembled. 'But I want—'

'It's of no moment what you want! We must do as *she* bids us, and try to please her!'

'*No!*' Elaine argued. 'What she bids us is wrong! If Father were here—'

Edmund said tightly, 'Father is not here.'

'But one day he will come home, and when he does, he will be angry to know that we have done wrong!' She turned and looked longingly at the grey sea, her eyes searching the horizon. 'He *will* come. He *will*!'

She had her back to Edmund and didn't see his face. But Jonas did, and understanding hit him hard. Elaine did not know what had happened to her and her brother. Edmund had grasped the truth, perhaps because he was older; but for the little girl, time had stopped on the day Sir Robert Leece had left to go to war.

Or perhaps on the night that Joanna had committed her appalling crime . . .

The two boys' gazes met, and Edmund saw that Jonas understood. Jonas said, 'She doesn't—' but Edmund snarled, 'Be silent!' He looked at his sister, who was still staring at the sea, and the dark hint of a grief that Jonas would never be able to comprehend shadowed his face.

'Elaine,' he said, much more softly. 'You must come away now. Don't fear; Father will be home soon.'

She blinked and turned to face him. 'Will he?'

'Yes. But now, you must come.'

She looked uncertainly at Jonas, then at her brother again. 'Have I done wrong?'

'No. You have been good. But we cannot stay any longer, or *she* might discover.'

Elaine nodded and slipped her small hand into his. Again she looked at Jonas, and seemed about to say something. But Edmund tugged at her fingers and she changed her mind.

And a moment later, the children were no longer there.

★ ★ ★

175

Jonas piled in at the back door and raced to find Rose.

'Mum! Where's Gil?'

'She came in about ten minutes ago.' Rose had stopped listening to the radio in case Alan phoned back. 'I called out to see if she wanted anything; she said she was fine, but she didn't sound it.'

'No. Right . . .' Jonas cast his gaze over the room, which was littered with scraps of leather, coils of twine and piles of dried leaves and flowers. It looked as if Rose was making some bizarre attempt at Christmas decorations. But the purpose of these, he knew, was a lot more serious.

He said, 'Mum, I've just met Robert Leece's children.'

Rose's eyes shot wide open. 'My God! *Where?*'

He told her, and described Elaine's warning.

'My God!' Rose said again. 'How on earth did Gil take it?'

'She didn't see them. She'd run off, you see, and . . .' Jonas was shaking by this time as reaction to the encounter set in, and his voice wasn't steady as he explained about Gil's challenge.

'She knows something's going on, and if we try to deny it, she'll just get more suspicious and hostile,' he said. 'Mum, we've got to tell her.'

'It could be dangerous!' Rose protested. 'Remember what your granfa said.'

'He hasn't rung again, has he?'

'No, not yet.'

176

'Then maybe I'd better call him and tell him what's happened.'

Rose hesitated a bare moment, then she nodded. 'All right. See what he says – and tell him to get home as quickly as he can!'

She carried on making the hasty garlands as Jonas hurried away to the hall. In less than a minute he was back.

'I got the answering service,' he said worriedly. 'Either he's switched the mobile off, or he's out of signal range. I left a message, but I don't know if he knows how to access it. He might not even realise I called.'

'Then we'll have to keep trying,' said Rose. 'Look, you'd better go upstairs and make sure Gil's all right. I'll carry on here.'

'OK.' He hesitated. 'Why are you making so many?'

She looked at him candidly. 'I honestly don't know. Your granfa said to do it, so I'm doing it. We'll find out why when he gets back. And let's hope that's soon.'

Gil was in her room, but she didn't want to talk to Jonas. If the door had had a lock, she would have locked it; as it was, when he came in she just sat on the window ledge with her back to him and refused to turn round. He tried to make friendly overtures, but all she said was, 'When you're ready to be honest with me, I'll talk; till then just go away and leave me alone.' Jonas gave up. His only consolation was that she seemed intent on staying put. All the same, when he went back to the ground floor he made sure he stayed in sight of the main staircase, in case she should try to sneak out.

The afternoon seemed to Jonas to last a month. He tried to help Rose, but he was so distracted that in the end she told him that he was more of a hindrance and to go and find something else to do. He tried the mobile number three more times, but each time the answering service cut straight in. That worried him. His grandfather had promised to call as soon as he knew what was wrong with the car – surely the breakdown service must have reached him by now? If he was still out of signal range, it could only mean that he was still stuck in the same place. By six he had not called, and with sunset only two hours away Jonas's worry started to swell into a deep, nagging fear.

Then at twenty past six, Alan rang.

'Granfa!' Jonas yelled down the phone in his relief. Chagrined, Alan told him that he had accidentally switched the mobile off and not realised it until a few minutes ago. And he did not have good news.

'The fuel pump's packed up, and it's going to be a garage job,' he said. 'It won't be done till late tomorrow at the very least. The breakdown people are arranging for a hire car to get me home, but I don't know when it'll be ready. I might not be back until very late. Is everything all right?'

'No,' said Jonas, 'it isn't.' He told him what had

happened, and why he now wanted Gil to be told the truth. 'It's the only way we'll get her to trust us,' he pleaded.

There was a long silence, then Alan replied, 'All right. I think under the circumstances you'd better. Ask your mother to talk to her with you.' Another hesitation. 'Has she done what I asked her?'

'She's been making garlands all day,' said Jonas. 'Other things, too; though she didn't tell me what they're for.'

'You don't need to know at the moment; what matters is that they're done. All right, Jonas; I'll ring off now, and get home as soon as I can.'

Rose was waiting when Jonas put the phone down. 'We can tell her,' Jonas said.

'Right. No time like the present, then. Can you face going through it again?'

He nodded, and together they headed for the stairs.

Gil was still sitting on the window ledge in her room. She looked round as they came in, and her expression became wary and hostile.

Rose didn't waste any time. 'Gil, we've got something to say to you.'

'Oh?' said Gil, with a hint of aggression. 'If it's about those horrible leaves—'

'It is, but that's only part of it. You think we've been hiding something from you. Well, you're right.'

Her bluntness took Gil aback. 'Oh . . .' she said again, in a changed tone. 'Then . . . you're going to own up about it, are you?' She shot a dagger glance at Jonas. 'It's about time.'

'Yes,' Rose agreed. 'It is.' She looked at Jonas. 'I think you'd better start by telling her exactly what happened last night.'

Steeling himself and keeping his voice as steady as he could, Jonas unfolded the story. As he talked, Gil's face tightened into a pinched, frozen mask. She was as still as stone, and when at last Jonas had told everything to the point where he had met his grandfather on the way back, a heavy silence fell.

Gil finally broke it. 'Jonas. Swear something to me.' There was an awful light in her eyes. 'Swear you're not making any of this up. Because if you are—'

'I'm not,' said Jonas solemnly. 'Every word of it's true. I swear.'

She began to tremble, and her mouth distorted to an ugly shape. 'I don't understand . . . Why don't I remember? *Why?*'

Rose leaned towards her and took hold of one hand. 'You've been made to forget, Gil,' she told her. 'The thing that attacked you—'

'The thing—' Hysteria tinged Gil's voice now. 'Jonas said, a grey woman . . . Who *is* she?'

'Ah . . . that's the other part of the story.' Rose squeezed her fingers, though there was no response. 'Do you feel up to hearing it, or—'

'I want to hear it! I want to know everything!'

So for the second time the whole story of Joanna was told. Again Gil listened in motionless silence, only her shocked eyes and dead-white face giving any clue to her feelings. Finally Rose told her about the earlier call from her father. Then Gil did react.

'No . . .' Her voice came out like a small, frightened mew and she pushed a clenched fist hard against her own mouth, as if to stop herself from either screaming or being sick. 'Biddy . . . oh, God . . .' With a jerky movement she jumped to her feet. 'I've got to go to London! I've got to *see* her! Aunt Rose, you've got a car—'

'Gil, there's no point!' Rose said. 'There'd be nothing you could do there, don't you understand? *We're* the only ones who can help both of you!'

'I don't believe you!' Gil flared. 'You're lying; you're making it up! *I don't believe anything you say any more!'* And she flung herself face down on her bed, sobbing violently.

Jonas made a move towards her, but Rose stopped him. 'Leave her be,' she whispered. 'It's shock, that's all; let her cry it out. Come on.' She drew him towards the door. 'We'll give her a bit of time on her own.'

They were both in the kitchen when Gil came downstairs half an hour later. Her face was still pale and her eyes red rimmed, but she had calmed down.

'I'm sorry,' she said stiffly before either Jonas or Rose could speak. 'I shouldn't have blown up like that.'

'Don't worry, pet.' Rose was sympathetic. 'It's hardly surprising.'

'Maybe, but . . .' Gil fidgeted awkwardly from one foot to the other. 'I've been thinking about what you told me. I still don't know if I believe it, but—'

'It's true!' Jonas interrupted.

'Shh, Jonas,' said Rose. 'Go on, Gil.'

'But . . . the only sensible thing to do is act as if it is true. Isn't it?'

'Yes,' Rose agreed, 'I think it is.'

'So if you say I can help Biddy, then I'll do what you want.' Gil's gaze ranged nervously round the kitchen and through the window, where the daylight was fading fast. 'Whatever it is.'

Rose sighed with relief. 'Thank you, Gil, love. I know it's all very strange and frightening, but believe me, it *is* the right decision. As soon as your Uncle Alan gets home, we'll talk about it properly, and he'll explain what has to be done.'

Gil nodded. 'All right, Aunt Rose. I . . . think I'll go back to my room now, if you don't mind.'

'Don't you want something to eat? I'm just going to get dinner on.'

'No, thanks. I'm not hungry. I'll probably have a sleep.'

'Well, that won't do you any harm. We'll call you when your uncle gets here. And Gil . . . I expect you found the pouch that he hung round your neck?'

Gil's eyes narrowed slightly. 'Yes . . .'

'Are you still wearing it?'

'Yes,' she repeated.

She was wearing a polo-necked sweater, so the pouch wasn't visible, but Rose knew she had to take her answer on trust. She smiled. 'Good. It'll protect you, you see. So . . . don't take it off, will you?'

'No,' said Gil. 'I won't.'

She went slowly out, shoulders drooping. When she was out of earshot Jonas said, 'Mum, what *has* got to be done? How dangerous is it going to be?'

Rose's brow furrowed, and he realised that she wasn't anything like as confident as she had pretended to Gil. 'I honestly don't know, Jonas,' she said. 'Your granfa has told me a bit, but not everything. Wait till he comes. That's all we can do.'

In her room, Gil lay on the bed with her arms behind her head, and watched the rectangle of the window darkening as dusk fell. She felt confused and shaky, and didn't quite know why she had lied when Rose asked her about the pouch. Maybe she shouldn't have thrown it away. Maybe it truly was a protection against Joanna . . . if, that was, Joanna really existed. If any of what she had heard had really happened.

She felt extraordinarily calm as she considered that. The one thing that struck a wrong note was the fact that she couldn't remember anything about it. Rose said that she had been made to forget; but Gil was sceptical. How *could* she have no memory of the red-haired children, let alone of going to the ruined church in the middle of the night? It was ridiculous. Things like that didn't happen.

She smiled thinly. She would wait; that was all. Wait until Alan came back and see what he had to say for himself. What would he want her to do? Something crazy, little doubt of that. Dance around waving those stupid garlands and making a total prat of herself, while he chanted some gibberish that was supposed to make Joanna Leece vanish in a puff of smoke. Gil giggled softly as the thought formed in her head: *As if something as dumb as that could make her disappear! They don't know anything at all.*

Wait, then. It was almost completely dark now, so it wouldn't be long before . . . She frowned, unable to work out what 'before' had to do with it, but the answer wouldn't come. Never mind. So Biddy had woken up, had she? (Biddy? Who was Biddy?) Mm. Interesting. Was it? Her arm itched . . .

The thin smile returned and Gil closed her eyes. But she had no intention of going to sleep.

Alan rang again while Rose was making lumpy mashed potato for their late meal and Jonas kept an eye on frying sausages. They both ran for the phone and Rose got there first.

'I'm at the garage getting the hire car now,' Alan said. 'As soon as the details are sorted out, I'll be on my way.'

'Thank heaven! How long do you think the journey'll take you?'

'It depends on the traffic — and whether I break any speed limits. I should be back by eleven.'

'Well, whatever you do, be careful, Dad!'

'I will, don't worry. Whatever *you* do, make sure Gil keeps that pouch round her neck. And she mustn't leave the house, under any circumstances!'

Rose hung up. She did not hear the soft click of the upstairs extension receiver being replaced. And she did not see the blank expression on Gil's face as she went very quietly back to her gable room.

In the gable, Gil sat down on the bed and the blankness in her face was replaced by a frown of intense concentration. Something she had to do. What was it? Biddy. Her little sister. It was something for Biddy. Wasn't it?

Inside her mind, a voice whispered, *Poor child, poor child . . .*

Biddy, yes. She was ill, and Gil wanted to help her.

Yes, Gillian. Together, we can help her. Come to me, and I will show you how . . .

She wanted to ring her parents, but by the time she picked up her mobile phone the impulse had faded. Why call them? *They* couldn't do anything. It was down to her, Gil, not them.

Help Biddy, Gillian. Help Biddy . . .

With a new clarity Gil realised what it was she had to

do. Knowing it was a huge relief; she suddenly felt energised and eager. She would have to wait for a while, because, again, things would be spoiled if Jonas and Rose found out what she was planning. But she could be patient. It was worth it.

She pocketed her phone, stood up again and went to the window. It was fully dark now, but a glimmer of grey light among the trees beyond the garden showed that the moon was rising. The first moon shadows were reaching out from the shrubbery. And there was another shadow, long and thin and with no obvious source, stretching from the garden gate towards the gable. It had some way to go before it reached the house. But when it did, everything would be all right. Everything.

Gil sat down on the window ledge and, with her gaze fixed on the slowly creeping shadow, prepared to wait.

Jonas and Rose ate their meal in virtual silence. They were both too tense to say much, and though Alan couldn't possibly get home for a good while yet they were constantly alert for the sound of a car engine. Neither ate much, either; Jonas washed up, and Rose, drying the last of the cutlery, stared the kitchen clock as if willing the hands to move faster.

'He said eleven,' Jonas reminded her. 'It's only just half-past ten.'

'He *might* be quicker.' Rose checked her watch to make sure that the clock was right. It was. 'I hope he isn't driving too fast. If he had an accident—' She swallowed. 'Maybe I should call him . . .'

'If he tries to answer the mobile while he's driving, he *will* have an accident,' said Jonas.

'Yes . . . yes, you're right. Look, I think I'll go and check on Gil. If she's awake, she might want to talk . . . It's got to be better than doing nothing . . .' The sentence tailed off. She went upstairs and Jonas wandered into the hall, where he opened the front door and stood staring out. The sky was clear of cloud and the wind had dropped completely, bringing a still and almost stifling summer warmth to the night. He looked for distant headlights but there were none. *Stop being impatient*, he told himself. *You're as bad as Mum.*

He heard Rose coming back down the stairs and turned. She was alone, and he said, 'Gil still asleep, is she?'

And in the instant before his mother answered, he registered the look on her face, and what it meant.

'No,' Rose said in a shaking voice. 'She's gone!'

14

It had been the most foolhardy and perilous thing Gil had ever done in her life, but now that it was safely over she felt elated. Lucky that she had noticed how the bathroom window opened above the small extension on the side of the house. Climbing out on to the sill had been nerve-racking, and when the moment had come to lower herself down to the extension roof, in the dark and with only the drainpipe to cling to, she had almost lost her nerve altogether. But the terror had passed; she had reached the roof, and though its slope had been steeper than she expected, she had managed to slither carefully to the edge, where she got a foothold against the guttering and could stop for a minute until her heart rate slowed down enough to tackle the next stage. Once she had plucked up the courage to ease herself over the edge of the roof, her feet were only a metre above the ground; all she had to do then was let go and drop to a safe landing. And no one in the house had suspected a thing.

Now she pushed the broken gate back and eased through it into the deserted lane. She knew where she wanted to go, even if she didn't quite know why, and she was not frightened. What was there to fear?

Something. Something very, very bad . . .

But the warning flickered and fled, and Gil turned in the direction of the ruined church. A sense of urgency was goading her, a need to hurry for some reason; her pace increased and by the time she approached the turning to the church she was almost running. A few minutes, just a few more, and everything would be all right . . .

The warning tried to come back again as she reached the lych gate, but, again, it didn't last long enough to affect her. She went through the gate and along the overgrown path to where the main doorway loomed like a black, open mouth. Inside the ruin it was quiet, peaceful. The moon lit the interior almost as brightly as day, and Gil picked her way towards the tomb of Robert Leece, eyes ranging now, seeking, eager.

And as she reached the stone monument, a soft voice away to her left spoke.

'Dear child . . . I have been waiting for you.'

A tiny part of Gil's mind screamed, *No, don't do it! Run away, run!* But the protest was too deeply buried and too weak. She turned round, slowly, and saw a tall grey column of mist swaying between two broken pillars a few paces away from her. It began to change and solidify; a human shape formed, a face framed by a headdress and veil. The face smiled sweetly . . . and Gil smiled too, as she took a slow step towards the figure that was now holding out its arms as if to embrace her . . .

★　★　★

'Welcome to the answering service for—'

'No, *no*!' Jonas slammed the phone receiver back on its rest. Granfa must have switched the mobile off while he was driving; sensible, of course, but right at this moment they needed to talk to him more than anything else in the world!

He swung round as Rose came running through the front door, holding a torch. Her face was white and strained; she said, 'She isn't in the garden. But Jonas, I found this!' She raised her free hand and he saw the pouch on its length of string. 'She must have taken it off and thrown it away. Oh, Jonas . . .'

'I'm going after her!' he said.

'No! You're not going alone – it's too dangerous! Anyway, the car's faster. We'll go together!'

The car's faster . . . But not, Jonas suddenly thought, as fast as a phone . . .

'Wait a minute!' He ran for the stairs, took them three at a time and raced to Gil's gable room. If her mobile wasn't there, then she must have it with her, and that was the quickest way to reach her.

In the space of a minute Jonas turned the room upside down, but Gil's mobile wasn't there. Praying she had it switched on, he leaped down the stairs again – then stopped as he realised that he didn't know her number. He had programmed it into his own mobile, but his grandfather had that, and he couldn't get through to him . . .

He heard the sound of Rose's car outside – and moments later the noise of another, more powerful engine. Headlights appeared, sweeping up the drive, and Jonas's heart gave a colossal thump of hope and excitement.

'*Granfa!*' He raced to meet the hire car as it came to a halt, and Alan got out. Jonas and Rose converged on him together and in a few breathless sentences told him what had happened.

'Granfa, where's my mobile?' Jonas finished urgently. 'I'll call her!'

Alan almost threw the mobile at him. 'Try and talk sense into her! I need to get some things together – Rose, come and help me!'

As they ran into the house Jonas switched his mobile on and feverishly called up Gil's number. It began to ring—

'Sweet child, I will comfort you. Come to me. Let me soothe you . . .'

Gil's mind was in a vague dream, and everything around her looked surreal and strange, almost as if she was drifting slowly through an underwater world. She felt happy, very happy . . . but somewhere she knew that things weren't quite right. Why weren't they right? What could possibly be wrong with this? The grey, smiling woman was her friend. Hadn't she said so? Hadn't she promised to help, to comfort, to make everything just the way it ought to be . . . ?

She took another step. The grey woman beckoned.

And from Gil's jacket came a shrill ringing sound.

Gil jolted violently – and her mind fragmented like shattering glass as Joanna's spell was broken. A whirl of wild, confused images hit her; night, the ruin, the towering grey shape, her phone— Before she even knew it she had plunged a hand into her pocket and snatched the mobile out.

'Gil! Gil, it's me, it's Jonas! Where are you?'

'Ahh . . .' Gil's mouth worked like a stranded fish.

'Gil, what's happening? Where are you?'

'J . . . Jonas . . .' Gil's eyes bulged as she stared fixedly at the phantom before her. *How did I get here? What have I done?* 'Jonas . . . help me . . .'

'Gil, are you at the church? You've got to get away from there!' Jonas's voice distorted as he yelled down the line.

No, Gillian. Don't run. I am here. You cannot leave me now.

'I w . . . oh, God, Jonas, she's—'

'Run, Gil, RUN! Meet us in the—' But the rest was drowned out as Joanna made a sudden lunge and Gil screamed. She stumbled backwards; in her terror her fingers accidentally broke the connection and the mobile went dead.

You cannot leave me, Gillian. I will always find you.

Terror turned to panic as Gil realised what she was facing, and with the speed of sheer desperation she rushed for the doorway. She burst out into the night and ran blindly, through the long grass, through the lych gate, out into the lane. *Run, run, RUN!* She didn't know where she was going; all she had was the driving, shrieking need to get away from the ruin, away from the horror; anywhere where the monstrous thing in the church wouldn't be able to find her—

Instinct made her race for cover, and the nearest cover was the belt of pine trees on the other side of the lane. She plunged towards them, her only thought to hide, and flung herself in among the crowding trunks, staggering and stumbling and rebounding through the trees in a desperate bid to reach safety.

Rose's little car bumped at bone-rattling speed up the rough drive from April House and turned on to the road. They would have to make a circuit to reach the lane that led to St. Osyth's; Rose stamped on the accelerator and the car careered erratically round the sweeping bends.

'If we meet any other traffic, at least we'll see their lights first!' she shouted above the engine noise. Jonas, in the back seat, clung to the door handle and peered through the windscreen past his mother and grandfather, straining for a glimpse of Gil as the hedges flashed past. He was crammed beside a bulging plastic dustbin bag. He didn't know what was in it and hadn't asked; he only hoped that Alan knew what he was doing.

The car took the next bend with a screech of tyres, and the headlights' stabbing beam showed the turning to the old church. Rose swung the wheel and they all but skidded off the road; then she trod hard on footbrake and clutch, and the car jolted to a stop outside the crumbling lych gate.

'Bring the bag!' Alan was already out of the car with Rose a pace behind, brandishing a torch as if it were a revolver. Jonas hefted the bag and followed them through the gate. He had a torch, too, but wasn't using it; the moon had cleared the treetops now and a cold, eerie glow suffused the churchyard, lighting the overgrown tombstones and showing the ruin in stark, clear silhouette.

'Should I try her phone again?' Jonas asked urgently as they approached the door arch.

'No,' said Alan. 'We might alert something else. Switch your torch off, Rose, and we'll go in quietly. Come on!'

The ruin's roofless walls closed round them with a vast sense of stillness that made Jonas shiver. There was absolute silence; no movement in the moon-shadowed corners, no sign of anyone or anything.

'She must be here!' he whispered in dismay.

Alan didn't comment but whispered back, 'We'll go further in.'

They picked a path through the rubble as quietly as they could, hearts thumping, eyes alert for the slightest movement. But by the time they reached Sir Robert Leece's tomb, they had found nothing.

'We couldn't have passed her on the road, could we?' Jonas asked incredulously.

'We'd *surely* have seen her.' Rose stared around, suppressing a shudder, and Alan glanced at the mobile in Jonas's hand. 'Perhaps you should call her again, Jonas. Not here, though; outside.'

Though none of them admitted it, they were all thankful to get out of the ruin. In the silver-lit churchyard Jonas called Gil's number again, and again it began to ring . . .

Gil had reached the dunes and had kept running until the soft sand underfoot slowed her and the running turned into an impossible effort. When that happened she dropped to her hands and knees in the sand, head hanging down and ribcage heaving with a mixture of fear and breathlessness. Crouching there, she gradually became aware that her surroundings had changed. The wind was sharp enough for her to feel its chill on her skin. There was a sense of huge openness. And there was the sound of the sea, waves hissing as they broke on the shoreline, and a deep, steady note underlying the hiss in a ceaseless, ominous moan.

Dazedly, she raised her head and looked around. The dunes and the beach beyond them were like a lunar landscape, silver and grey and about as desolate as it was possible to be. The tide was low but coming in, and though the waves were small and sluggish, to her scrambled mind they looked menacing. Gil tried to think clearly, but her only coherent thought was that she had escaped from the ruined church and, whatever happened she must stay as far away from it as she possibly could. *The beach is the safest place. I'll stay on the beach, then maybe she won't see me . . .*

She was trying to huddle against a dune and make herself as small as possible when she heard the muffled ringing of her mobile a short way off.

Befuddled, Gil looked around, then saw the mobile lying in the sand a couple of metres away. She grabbed it and whispered, 'H . . . hello . . .?'

'Gil?'

'Jonas!' She shut her eyes in relief.

'Where are you?'

'On the . . . On the beach somewhere, I think. I ran away . . .'

'Are you all right?' Jonas asked urgently.

'Y . . . yes. I'm OK. But I'm *scared*.'

In the churchyard, Alan grasped Jonas's arm. 'Find out where she is. A landmark, anything.'

Jonas nodded. 'Gil, can you see anything that'll help us find you? Rocks, trees, whatever?'

Taking a tight hold on her terror, Gil peered round the edge of the dune. The full moon hung high overhead, blotting out the stars and turning the sky to a strange, flat pewter colour. Its light made everything look featureless and blank. But one of the groynes was longer than the rest . . . and just behind it the pines encroached on the beach in a sort of spur . . .

She garbled the landmarks and Jonas nodded to his grandfather. 'I know where she is. There's a short cut, through the trees – I can get to her in five minutes.'

'Good! Tell her you're on your way.' Jonas did, cut the phone connection and was about to sprint off when Alan added, 'And bring her back here.'

'*What?*' Jonas was astonished. 'No way! Mum can drive the car round, get to the beach from the road and—'

Alan said, 'Jonas.' And his tone stopped Jonas in mid-protest.

'Listen to me,' his grandfather went on. 'If we're going to end this – and I mean *end* it, once and for all – then Gil must come back to the church.'

'But that thing – Joanna—'

'Will win this battle, unless you do as I say.' Alan glanced uneasily up at the sky. 'The full moon at this time of year is known as the Hunter's Moon, and people used to believe that it had a powerful influence.' Now his gaze returned to Jonas's. 'I'm asking you to trust me, and do exactly what I tell you. Because Joanna is hunting tonight, and it could be our last chance to stop her. The last chance for Biddy – and for Gil.'

They stared at each other, and Jonas saw a strange, burning light in his grandfather's eyes. Something . . . fanatical? No, he realised. Desperate was a better word. Desperate and, almost, pleading. *The last chance*, he had said. And the thought came to Jonas that Alan had waited a very long time for this chance. The chance to avenge his brother . . .

As if from a long way off, he heard himself say, 'I trust you, Granfa.'

The look in Alan's eyes changed. He said softly, 'Thank you . . .'

Then Jonas was gone, sprinting towards the lane.

Jonas emerged from the belt of pine trees and climbed to the top of a sand hill, staring along the beach as his eyes accustomed themselves to the tricky light. He knew roughly where Gil should be, but there was no sign of her, and he cupped both hands to his mouth and called her name. The sharp *kee-yip* of an owl answered somewhere high in the trees. Then, from behind a dune about thirty metres away, a figure cautiously emerged.

'Gil!' Jonas slithered down the hill and ran to her, grabbing her in a crushing hug.

She hugged him back. 'Oh, Jonas . . . am I glad to see you!'

'Why did you *do* it?' he asked. 'Going off like that—'

'I couldn't stop myself! I can't even really remember doing it; it was all like a dream.' She swallowed. 'Till my mobile rang. It snapped me out of it. If you hadn't called then . . .'

She started to shiver violently and he said, 'Don't think

about it. You're OK; that's what matters. Come on. Let's get back to Granfa.'

Gil looked fearfully around. 'I'd rather stay here . . . What if she's out there, waiting for me?'

'She isn't.'

'You don't know that!' Gil shrank back among the dunes. 'I'm *scared*, Jonas!'

'All right, all right . . .' He tried to think of something that would reassure her, and remembered the pouches. He should have brought Gil's discarded one with him . . . But he still had his own, and he took it off. 'Have this. It'll protect you, just like it protected me.'

She looked doubtful, but let him loop the thong around her neck. 'Better?' he asked. 'Good! Come on, then.'

They moved out from the dunes and back towards the pines. At the edge Gil hung back, reluctant to go among the trees, but Jonas took a tight hold of her hand and led her in. Sand gave way to a carpet of pine needles under their feet and the wind hissed softly in the branches overhead; Jonas paused to judge his direction, then veered off to the left.

Suddenly Gil hissed, '*What's that?*'

'What?' He looked round quickly and saw her pointing.

'Over there . . . Look!'

Between two tree trunks about ten metres away, a grey mist was forming. For a moment Jonas tried to tell himself that it was a trick of the moonlight. But it was solidifying – and taking on a human shape.

He tightened his grip on Gil's hand and shouted, '*Run!*'

They ran, crashing and stumbling among the trees. Behind them the mist swirled, vanished—

And reappeared directly in front of them.

Gil screamed and Jonas yelped, and they both flailed into a skidding turn. But even as they raced away from the phantom, there was a flicker in the air and it was in front of them again. Its shape was definitely human now, and they could see the first faint traces of a face. Again Gil and Jonas turned and ran; again the figure was suddenly there in their path. The face was clearer, and it was smiling a horrifying smile.

'She's c-closer each time,' Gil whispered, clinging to Jonas's arm. 'We can't get away from her . . . oh God, Jonas, what are we going to do?'

Jonas's mouth was too dry for speech and, anyway, he had no answer. They stumbled back, turned again, ran again—

From somewhere to their right a voice cried: '*Over here!*'

Elaine was there, peering round a tree trunk and beckoning urgently. They swerved towards her just as the grey mist materialised once more, and they both heard Joanna's shrill cry of rage as they dodged past her and raced towards Elaine. The little girl vanished before they reached her, but another voice hissed: '*To me!*

Quickly!' and they glimpsed the gleam of Edmund's red hair in the darkness, to their left this time. Again Joanna appeared; but again Elaine's cry warned them and they changed direction in time. It was as if the children could predict Joanna's every move; flickering and darting, they guided Gil and Jonas on a crazy, zigzag course among the trees, until they were breathless and totally confused. But it seemed they had confused Joanna, too. She was still pursuing them, but each time she was further away, as if she could no longer be sure of where they were. Then the trees thinned out, the moonlight brightened – and Gil and Jonas ran out on to a tarmaced road.

Gil slithered to a halt, panting, and stared around. Nothing looked familiar, and she gulped down enough breath to gasp, 'Where are we?'

'I think I know.' Jonas was breathing hard, too. 'It's our lane, but further up. The old church is about two hundred metres that way.' He pointed to their left, then took hold of her hand again. 'Come on! Let's find Mum and Granfa!'

She was about to go with him, but abruptly froze. 'Wait a minute . . . What's that?' She pointed down the road, and to his horror Jonas saw what looked like grey smoke drifting out from the trees about fifty metres ahead of them, coiling, taking shape . . .

Behind them, Edmund's voice said, 'This way!'

Gil yelped with renewed shock, and they both swung

round. Edmund had emerged from the trees, with Elaine by his side. Their eyes were huge and wide, and they gestured frantically to the undergrowth on the other side of the road.

'We know another way,' Edmund said. 'Follow us. Hurry!'

Gil and Jonas didn't hesitate. As the children glided into the undergrowth and disappeared, they followed. There was a tangle of bushes, and beyond them a half collapsed stone wall. An ancient yew tree was growing against the wall, and amongst its dark foliage they saw Edmund crouching on the wall top and beckoning. They climbed over, ignoring scraped hands and legs, and dropped down into what felt like a cold, dank cave where the yew boughs arched over and almost touched the ground. Ducking, they pushed their way through the branches, emerged into open ground – and Gil stopped, staring.

'Look where we are!'

Jonas had already seen for himself. The ruined church towered ahead of them, a great black bulk against the pewter sky. They must have approached it from the far side of the graveyard, Gil thought, and all the fear associated with it abruptly came back.

'Jonas, I don't want to go back there!'

Jonas didn't, either, but before he could agree aloud, Edmund and Elaine reappeared. The moonlight had drained them of colour except for the flame-red of their hair; for the first time they truly looked like ghosts. Elaine said, 'Don't be afraid, Gillian!' and Edmund added to Jonas, 'Your grandfather and mother are in the church; I have seen them. But don't go in by the great door. There's another way; we can show you.'

'Hear that, Gil?' said Jonas. 'Granfa and Mum are there. Come on – the sooner we find them, the sooner we'll be safe.'

Gil was still scared, but she didn't have a better suggestion. They followed Edmund through the long, damp grass towards the ruin. The ancient walls seemed to frown down, and when they rose high enough to block out the moon, Gil gave a shiver that had nothing to do with cold.

At one corner of the building was another tree, growing out of the wall, and Edmund said, 'It hides the doorway that leads to the sacristy, where the holy vessels were kept. *She* does not like to linger here.' He almost, but not quite, smiled at them. 'Go, now. God speed you!'

Jonas lifted back the branches and saw the small, low doorway, with open space beyond. He turned to thank Edmund, but the boy and his sister were gone.

'All right?' Jonas squeezed Gil's hand.

'Yeah. All right.'

They ducked their heads and went into the church.

Under the cavernous shelter of the yew tree, Elaine looked up at her brother with solemn eyes.

'We shouldn't have lied,' she said miserably. 'It is sinful to lie . . . Father has said so.'

'We had no choice.' He didn't meet her gaze. 'It's the only way, Elaine. It's the only chance we have.'

15

At the turning to the ruined church Rose peered anxiously up and down the lane, then ran back to the lych gate, where Alan was opening the hatchback of the car.

'Still no sign of them,' she reported. '*Surely* Jonas must have found her by now?'

'Give them a bit longer,' said Alan. He took two plastic cans and a bundle of old rags out of the car and set them carefully down on the ground. 'I'm going to take these into the church, then I think everything's ready.'

Rose looked worriedly at the cans. 'Dad, is this really going to work? If anything went wrong . . .'

'So long as we're careful, the worst that could happen is that we fail to get rid of Joanna Leece,' Alan said grimly. 'And believe me, Rose, I'm going to be careful.' He met her eyes. 'I love Jonas too, you know. I won't let anything happen to him – or to Gil.'

Rose wished she felt as confident as he sounded, but didn't say so. 'Do you want any more help?' she asked.

'No, I can manage. Go and keep watching. I won't be long.'

He hurried off through the gate and Rose went back to the lane, where she stood fidgeting from foot to foot and staring into the darkness. Alan came back soon afterwards, and she said, 'Still nothing!'

'All right. We'll give them a few more minutes, then we'll go and look for them.' He put a hand on her shoulder, trying to be reassuring. 'Don't worry, love. They'll be here.'

Gil and Jonas eased through a small archway into the main section of the ruin, and peered around. The church looked empty, and moonlight slanting in at the gaping windows cast deceptive and disturbing shadows. Gil didn't want to look at the tomb of Robert Leece away to one side, but she forced herself to glance towards it, just in case. Nothing moved there, and she let her breath go thankfully.

But there was no sign of Alan and Rose.

'Granfa?' Jonas called softly. 'Granfa! Mum! Where are you?'

No answer came out of the gloom. Frowning, Jonas moved further into the church, Gil following closely and looking over her shoulder every few seconds.

Then in the darkest corner Jonas saw movement. An arm, beckoning . . . 'They they are.' Relief filled him, and he turned, hurrying towards what he could now make out as a shadowy human figure. Gil was about to follow – but stopped as doubt crept into her mind. *Were* Alan and Rose there? All she could see was a shadow, without detail. It could be anything. It could be—

'Jonas!' Suddenly the doubt became a certainty and she sprang after him. She was too late. The shape moved so fast that Jonas had no chance to avoid it. Gil heard his yell of shock, and then he was sprawling full-length on the floor, with the grey figure of Joanna Leece looming over him. A gaunt hand snaked out and caught hold of Jonas's arm, and he yelled again as nails like talons raked his skin from elbow to wrist.

Gil didn't believe what she was seeing – Jonas was protected; how could Joanna attack him? Then in an instant she remembered. Jonas was no longer wearing his pouch on its thong. He had given it to her on the beach when she was frightened – he *had* no amulet against Joanna; he was totally vulnerable!

She didn't stop to think, but screamed, '*No!*' and hurled herself across the space between them, snatching at the pouch as she ran. The thong broke, and Gil flung the pouch with all her strength straight at Joanna's head. In her panic the throw was wild; appalled, she saw the pouch fly past a metre from its target. Joanna turned to face her, snarling, and Gil's momentum took her careering to where Jonas sprawled. She tripped over his outstretched legs and crashed to the floor beside him with an impact that knocked the breath out of her lungs. They rolled, ending up in a breathless tangle against the stump of a stone pillar; Gil started to struggle upright – and froze as she saw a pool of mist curling on the floor in front of her, and rising . . .

Her head jerked up, and she looked into the evilly beautiful face of Joanna Leece.

The phantom smiled a terrible smile, and a grey hand reached towards them. In her head, Gil heard the chilling voice: '*Foolish children . . . such foolish children . . .*'

Jonas gasped, and Gil knew he was hearing it, too. He was gripping his arm where Joanna's nails had slashed it, and blood seeped through his clamped fingers.

'*Ah, but you will not run from me now, will you? You cannot run. I know. Come to me, dear children. Come to me . . .*'

Gil could feel her mind fogging, as if she were falling asleep, and the whispering, cajoling voice was impossible to resist. '*Come to me,*' Joanna commanded. '*Dear children . . .*'

Very slowly, Gil stood up. She didn't want to, she *didn't*, and when one foot started to move forward she struggled with all her willpower to stop it. But her muscles wouldn't obey her.

'Fight it, Gil!' Jonas gasped. 'Try to fight it!' He had clamped both hands against his own skull in an attempt to shut out the deadly voice. Gil struggled to stay still, but her foot kept on moving. One step, just one, and the grey apparition would be able to reach out and touch her . . .

'I c . . . can't fight . . .' she moaned. 'She . . . won't let me . . . oh, Jonas . . .'

'*Come, children. Come.*'

Jonas's throat worked convulsively. He was trying to shout, Gil thought; and she wanted to shout too; shout and yell, *anything* that might break the spell and set her mind free. *Help!* her mind was screaming; *Uncle Alan, Aunt Rose, help us!* But she couldn't make the sound come; her tongue wouldn't work and her throat was closing from fear and the power of Joanna's will.

'There, now. I will soothe you both. Give your minds to me. Give your minds and your thoughts and your strength. There is nothing to fear. Nothing. Nothing . . .'

Jonas sighed happily, like someone drifting away into a pleasant dream. Gil was drifting, too. She wasn't afraid any more. *Joanna is our friend*, she thought vaguely. *She will help us. All we have to do is give up trying . . .*

'I'm not waiting any longer.' Rose's voice was sharp with tension. 'They should have been back by now – I'm going to the beach to look for them!'

She turned to go – and Elaine materialised in front of her.

'Ahh!' Rose's cry was shrill in the quiet as she jumped back, and Alan said, 'Good God!'

'Wh-who are you?' Rose stammered, but before Elaine could reply, Alan ran forward. 'You're Elaine, aren't you? Sir Robert Leece's child?'

'She's my sister,' said another voice, and Edmund appeared. Rose clutched Alan's arm, her mouth wide open, but Edmund ignored her and looked challengingly at Alan. 'I told her not to come to you. But . . .' His eyes narrowed and his look became intense. 'I know who you are. I know what became of your brother.'

Rose gasped, but Alan waved her to silence. His own eyes were alight with emotion and he said, 'Then you know what will happen to Gil and her sister, if we don't end this once and for all.' Edmund frowned, and Alan added harshly, 'I failed before, because I was too young and inexperienced to know what was happening. But I understand now. I've spent all my life finding out what I should have done all those years ago, and I'm going to do it – so don't try to stop me!'

'Don't stop him, Edmund!' Elaine pleaded. 'Perhaps Father sent him!' She turned huge, eager eyes on Alan. '*Did* our father send you to help us? He has gone away over the sea, and we have been waiting for him to come back and make everything right again. But he has not come yet. Did he send you in his place?' She sighed. 'We have been waiting for so long . . .'

Rose made a choking sound and put a fist to her mouth, and Alan's eyes softened with pity.

'Maybe your father did send me, Elaine,' he said gently. 'And if—'

He broke off as Edmund said, '*Oh*—'

The boy's outline shivered, wavered, then returned to normal. But his expression had changed.

'In the church!' he said. 'They are there. And *she*—'

'What? But we were waiting here for them!'

'We led them by another way.' Edmund looked quickly at his sister and seemed to make a decision. 'No more deceiving,' he said. 'It's like lying – it's a sin!' Squaring up, he faced Alan once more. 'We must help Jonas! We must help Gillian!'

And with a dizzying flicker, the children were skimming away, speeding towards the church.

Gil was dreaming that she was floating on the sea. The water felt warm, and everything around her shimmered with wonderful shades of green and blue. Jonas was somewhere nearby, she knew; she wondered if he could see the colours, too, but it was too much effort to turn her head and ask him. She was *so* sleepy. Hardly any energy at all, and the little she had was fading, fading away . . .

She heard the shouting voices with a vague part of her mind. At first they seemed to have nothing to do with her, but when a powerful and familiar smell suddenly assaulted her nostrils, it was such a contrast with the pleasant feelings that it momentarily jolted her out of her trance. And the moment was enough.

Petrol – what on earth—?

Someone yelled her name, and reality came back with a slamming force that made Gil leap to her feet before anything could stop her. Her eyes snapped open, the petrol smell was suddenly, violently stronger, and she saw a figure rushing at her, brandishing what looked like a large bunch of leaves.

'*Gil! Catch it!*' Rose's arm went back and she hurled the garland. Gil was too confused to catch it, but she flung her hands up instinctively and the garland, unravelling as it went, tangled over her arms. Another garland flew through the air, and Joanna Leece recoiled with a shriek as it landed in the spot where she had been hovering.

'Get one to Jonas!' Rose yelled. 'Help him!'

Gil swung round and saw Jonas lying prone among the rubble two metres from her. He wasn't moving; he was unconscious; she struggled to make sense of what was happening, but her mind was still confused and foggy. *Help him* – How? What was she supposed to do?

'The garland!' Rose screamed. 'Give him the garland!'

At last Gil understood, and she snatched up the garland on the floor. But as her fingers touched it there was another scream, raging, demented, inside her head:

'*No! No! NO! I WILL NOT ALLOW IT!*'

A sensation like a massive electric shock went through Gil as Joanna called on all her supernatural strength to break through the garland's protection. Gil was hurled backwards, arms windmilling; she cannoned into the broken pillar, rebounded and lost her balance. As she fell, Joanna's figure began to stretch and tower and darken, and her voice was an unholy roar battering into Gil's mind:

'YIELD! YIELD! I WILL NOT BE THWARTED!'

And amid the mayhem another voice, young and clear, called, 'Elaine! To me!'

The two Leece children came running from the direction of the main doorway, and as they did so, a powerful torch beam stabbed through the church like a theatre spotlight. Jagged shadows leaped, and in the glare Gil saw Rose throwing more garlands.

'Elaine!' Edmund cried. 'You know what we must do!'

The garlands landed – and the two children began to spin. Faster and faster, until in seconds they had become tiny, whirling tornadoes that whipped up gusts of wind and hurled dust and debris in all directions. The garlands were hurled, too, coiling and twisting on the floor – and in a stunning moment Gil realised what they were doing. This was Edmund and Elaine's way of gathering up the garlands – they were controlling them, making them jump and slide and coil themselves into a circle that surrounded Joanna and her victims—

'Gil! Jonas!' Alan's voice bellowed. 'Get ready to run!'

Gil flung another look at Jonas. He still wasn't moving, and she screamed back, 'He's unconscious! I can't—'

The words choked off as another light, hotter and brighter than the torch, flared into life. Fire – it lit Alan's haggard face and she saw the blazing, oil-soaked rag in his hand. He was going to throw it – but Jonas wasn't moving, and Gil couldn't carry him—

The burning rag soared up and out, and as it hit the floor, a column of fire went up with a deep, explosive *whoof*. In less than a second the column was a wall, spreading, racing in both directions, forming another circle, wider than the garlands; trapping them—

Joanna Leece uttered an unearthly shriek of rage and horror that nearly burst Gil's eardrums. She, too, started to whirl, and Gil's mind felt the shattering power of her fury. But there was fear in the fury now. She had lost her hold on Gil, lost control, and Gil took a huge breath and yelled with all the strength she had:

'*Uncle Alan! HELP!*'

Thick, acrid smoke caught in her throat and she doubled over, coughing. The circle of fire was complete, roaring higher; then the first of the garlands caught light, and a river of flame hissed towards her. She couldn't scream again; she felt as if she was choking – until suddenly a figure was bursting through the fire wall and running towards her.

'*Come on!*' With astonishing strength and agility Alan heaved Jonas over his shoulder, then grabbed hold of Gil's arm. 'Just take a deep breath, and *run!*'

He rushed back at the fire like a charging bull and Gil went helter-skelter with him. The blazing wall came at them; she shut her eyes in terror, but couldn't stop. There was a surge of searing heat – then they were through the barrier and Gil collapsed to her hands and knees as Rose flung soaking wet towels over them all.

'Out!' Alan shouted. 'Leave everything; just *go*!'

Jonas was groaning and starting to stir, but his grandfather didn't wait for him to come round; only hefted him again and ran, with Rose towing Gil a pace behind him. The main doorway was ahead of them, a safe haven; by the time they reached it Gil could feel the fire's heat on her back. Alan ran outside, but as Rose followed Gil let go of her hand and stopped, turning to look back. What she saw in that moment would haunt her dreams for a long, long time. For there in the circle of fire was a towering grey shadow that writhed and twisted in a mad parody of a dance. Joanna was struggling to escape – but there was no escape for her. And to one side of her, two small, red-haired figures stood hand in hand, their heads high and their stances proud and upright. Through the smoke, Gil saw Edmund and Elaine smile . . .

'Gil, get clear of the door!' Rose had come back and was pulling her forcibly away. Dazed, Gil stumbled after her; they ran along the path to the lych gate where Alan waited – and as they joined him, a thin, eerie wail rose up into the night. They all heard it, even Jonas, who was now raising his head from the ground where Alan had laid him. And they all saw the flickering light – far paler and colder than the light from the fire – that rose in a spiral above the ruin, shivered, and faded to nothing.

For nearly a minute there was silence but for the distant crackling of the flames inside the church; though even that was gradually fading as the fire died down. Then Alan said,

'She's gone. She's really gone . . .'

There was a catch in his voice, and Gil looked at him. If anyone had told her before tonight that Alan Granger could cry, she wouldn't have believed it. Now, though, she did.

She turned away to save his feelings, and knelt down beside Jonas, who was trying to sit up. He blinked at her, then said groggily, 'What happened . . . ?'

'That's a corny movie line!' Gil nearly laughed but stopped herself, in case it turned into hysterics.

'Yeah . . . so I'm corny.' He screwed his eyes up. 'I've got a hell of a headache.'

'Too many late nights!' Why was she being so flippant? Relief, that was the obvious answer. *Either make jokes or burst into tears, Gil. Your choice.*

Alan joined them then. He gave Jonas a rapid but professional examination and said, 'Nothing that a day or two's rest won't cure.' He paused. 'How much can you remember?'

'Not a lot,' Jonas admitted. 'But I heard what you said, Granfa. Has Joanna *really* gone?'

'Oh, yes.' Alan hunched his shoulders and shivered. 'She died by fire all those centuries ago, and it was the one thing she truly feared, because she knew she couldn't withstand it a second time. It was the one thing that could finally destroy her. So the garlands trapped her . . .

and the flames did the rest.' Now he managed a smile. 'What you two did took a lot of courage.'

'And some stupidity,' said Gil in a small voice. 'If I hadn't gone off like that . . .'

'You couldn't help yourself, Gil. Joanna was controlling you.' Alan straightened. 'But she'll never control anyone else again.' His voice hardened. '*Never*.'

Rose came over. 'It'll be dawn soon,' she said. 'The moon's setting. Shall we go home?'

Gil nodded. She longed to sleep – real sleep this time, not the deadly, trance-like state that Joanna had lured her into. She helped Jonas to his feet and they all climbed into the car. As Rose started the engine, she thought: *There's so much to say. So much, still, to understand.* But tomorrow would be time enough for that.

Rose drove back to April House very slowly, and by the time the car pulled up outside the front door there was a distinct glimmer of light in the easterly sky. Gil shivered as she waited for Alan to unlock the door, then she walked unsteadily in, blinking in the hall's bright light. Everything looked so normal. It was almost like a dream . . .

Rose had just said, 'Does anyone want a hot drink before we all go to bed?' when the phone rang.

They all started, and fear leaped in Gil's heart. But Alan was smiling at her, as if he knew something she didn't. He said, 'Why don't you answer it, Gil?'

She picked up the receiver, aware that her pulse was starting to race. 'Hello?'

'Gil?'

'Dad! What—'

Her father's voice was brimming with excitement as he interrupted. 'Oh, Gil, love! I'm sorry to wake everyone so early, but Mum and I couldn't wait till proper morning! Gil, Biddy's come round! She's going to be all right!'

Though the others couldn't hear what he said, they all saw Gil's face light up like a star. 'Dad!' she cried. 'Oh, *Dad*!'

'It happened just an hour ago,' Mr Chandler went on. 'She started to stir suddenly, then she just opened her eyes, and she *knew* us! She's very weak, of course she is; but the doctors are certain she'll make a full recovery!'

The phone was grabbed from him then by Gil's mother, who was laughing and crying at the same time. Gil would never properly remember what they all said to each other; it was just a babbling confusion, with everyone taking their turn to say all kinds of foolish, happy things. But towards the end of the call, Gil spoke to her mother again. Mrs Chandler had calmed down a bit, and she said,

'Gil, love . . . are *you* all right? I mean . . . *really*?'

Had she guessed? Gil wondered. There was no way of knowing . . . and, as yet, she couldn't decide whether she would ever tell her parents the whole truth. She looked round at the other three. Alan was smiling (though perhaps it was a faintly sad smile?) and Rose's expression was downright soppy. While Jonas . . .

Jonas saw her studying his face, and winked.

Gil turned back to the phone. 'Yes, Mum,' she said. 'I think I'm just about as all right as it's possible to be.'

Jones saw her make up her face, and with a
Continental shrug of the shoulders Miss Mildred, and
these two are just not prepared to type and left her.